T0196873

FINDING FAIRWAYS AND DREAMS

Conversations between the Third
Green and the Fourth Tee

DOUG EVANS

BALBOA.
PRESS

A DIVISION OF HAY HOUSE

Balboa Press books may be ordered through booksellers or by contacting:

Balboa Press
A Division of Hay House
1663 Liberty Drive
Bloomington, IN 47403
www.balboapress.com.au
1 (877) 407-4847

Print information available on the last page.

ISBN: 978-1-5043-1150-2 (sc)
ISBN: 978-1-5043-1151-9 (e)

Balboa Press rev. date: 11/23/2017

THE WARM UP

A golf ball rolling into the cup makes a unique sound that is immediately recognisable to golfers and those who follow this remarkable game. When you hear that sound, although it may signal numerous outcomes and elicit varied emotions of wildly swinging range, interestingly, none of them are ever negative. It may be an exultant celebration of success in the case of a birdie or eagle, or calming relief if you have made an exceptional par save, perhaps even the end of a disastrous hole, but at least it is over and it is positive because the torture has finally stopped and you can move on to the next hole with hope and restored expectation. I don't know of many other things in this world you can rely upon to make you feel positive, every time, irrespective of the different paths, methods and results.

I tell you this because it's an example of how Davey Neilson, known to all as Super Caddy, encourages his player. Other caddies may say things like "put a good stroke on it", "remember it breaks two cups left", or "focus on your line", those are technical things and important, but Davey would say "let me hear that sound". It's much more emotive and helps the player lock into the positivity of a powerful feeling and concentrate on the end result and not the process. It may be that I respond better to kinaesthetic and auditory cues, but I always found it very motivating, and it allowed a freedom to the flow of the shot. The other type of directions are instructive and focused on the next stroke, and if you don't manage it you have failed, but with Dave's quiet request, you know eventually you will succeed in giving him what he wants no matter how many putts it takes. It draws on years of positive memories and visualisation, without the pressure of delivering a technically perfect effort.

There's enough failure and losing in the game of golf as it is, a pursuit where total perfection is never achievable and complete mastery is unattainable, despite the tantalising glimpses we get occasionally. Dave knows this so he will look for as many small wins as possible for future reference. That is part of his innate genius, he understands people and how we work.

I want to share with you the story of how Super Caddy works his magic. I had a revelation suddenly one morning when I realised that his observational logic and calm advice and what we learn from the challenges in golf apply beautifully to our dreams and aspirations and indeed our whole lives, and not just on the fairways and greens. We can all benefit by making this connection. I suspect he always knew that, the rest of us just needed to catch up…..

1ˢᵀ HOLE

The first hole of any round is like your teenage years. You start out with endless possibilities and enthusiasm, just happy to be out here, fresh, strong, actively preparing, absorbing the experience and excitedly looking forward to what is ahead. Not worried about missteps as there is plenty of time left to make up for mistakes and bad decisions.

Dave was born in Ballarat, and his childhood was a typical country Australian upbringing with decent, hardworking parents. His dad was a skilled and respected tradesman. His mum was the touchstone for family standards, maintaining the household while also working long hours in small businesses. A couple of younger sisters who looked up to their big brother completed the immediate family unit, although as was the norm for that era, Dave enjoyed a large extended family in nearby towns with whom he spent the kind of time that none of us seem to have anymore. Victorians, especially in country areas, are sports mad, with Australian Rules football and, to a lesser extent, cricket being the main devotions. I use that word deliberately because as someone from another state, I am continually amazed and impressed how the dedication of Victorians to their AFL teams has an unashamedly religion-styled faithfulness and commitment.

For a small regional area, Ballarat boasts a staggering number of successful well-known people, which is quite disproportionate to city and metropolitan ratios. For example, opera singers David Hobson and Jacqueline Dark, and musician David Hirschfelder were born there. Four prime ministers (Deakin, Curtin, Scullin, and Menzies), businessmen (including Reginald Ansett), multiple premiers and politicians, military leaders, academics, scientists, and religious leaders originate from the area. I suspect, though, the sports stars from Ballarat stir more passion in the average person. Tony Lockett, Drew Petrie, and Mick Malthouse are a few AFL examples. Steve Moneghetti (marathon running), Ray Borner (basketball), Peter Blackburn (badminton), and Russell Mark (trap shooting) are all Olympians with a Ballarat connection. This is a small sample; there are so many more people who have a history with Ballarat and have gone on to great things.

This is also true for many country towns in Australia, and I have heard many theories about why this happens, including fewer distractions for young people, the powerful desire to move out of the small towns, the hardworking, physical culture, respect for traditions and family, and community support. I am sure all of these have an impact, but I like to think that the main driver is the higher emphasis placed on values and ethics, and how these are instilled in young people in country towns. And the long list of successful people from Ballarat suggests there is an extremely high emphasis on all those elements in this town.

It is especially important and evident in sports. I am sure Dave was schooled in the merit of these attributes, and this helped develop his character. It is interesting that he made his way into the world of golf. In my view, golf is one of the last sports where integrity and sportsmanship are hallmarks of the game, and respect for the history and legacy of the sport is preserved and promoted. In what other sport does a player call a penalty on himself or herself? In some sports, it is even encouraged, rewarded, and celebrated when a player deliberately flaunts the rules to win a penalty or gain an advantage. I am sure it is even practised! Some players have made a lucrative career out of this tactic. But in golf, if you cheat or even bend the rules, it can end your career. The truth and honesty of that have always resonated deeply with me.

An example of an early lesson in values for Dave came when he used to go to work with his dad on school holidays. His father was a plasterer back in the days when they still made the ornate cornices themselves at home, and the work on-site was predominantly done by hand. So skills honed over a long apprenticeship were crucial; there were no shortcuts. On one hot, dusty Friday afternoon, long after the other tradies had left; Dave and his dad were finishing a section behind a wall in the kitchen pantry that was to be later covered with timber cladding. Being a young man, eager to finish work and head out for the night with his friends, Dave was keen to get home to clean up. He couldn't understand why they had to be so particular with finishing off this section as it was going to be covered up later. He put this to his father rather impatiently.

"No one is going to know or even care, Dad."

There was an empty silence for what seemed like minutes to Dave but was most likely only ten or twenty seconds. Finally, his father spoke quietly in a tone that accentuated the power of each word. "That isn't exactly true, son. I will know, and so will you. And I don't want to feel that I cheated the owner every time I drive past this house, even though he will never know. I most certainly care about that. How about you?"

There is real momentum in a question like that at the end of a sentence, throwing it to the other person to decide the next action. It could produce self-analysis, some soul-searching, deep thought about the future implications and applications to other situations, and even change an attitude.

Or maybe it would simply confirm the decision that he doesn't care, and that's the end of it. But it puts the responsibility on the recipient of the question. Invariably, when Dave is caddying, he will use this technique. He may say,

"If it were me playing the shot, I would do this. What do you want to do?" Or, "The risk is too high to take on that shot. There are other options, but it's your call. Are you willing to take that risk?" Another variation is used when he seeks conviction from the player and a commitment to the shot choice: "Is that the shot you see in your head? Are you happy with that club choice?" He rarely gives straight directions unless it is required. It's as plain as that: describe the situation, offer alternatives, ask for a decision, and demand a commitment, clearly reminding the player where the responsibility lies. If there's no decision, Dave starts the process over again. It is straightforward but so powerful.

I often wonder if he learned that consciously from his own experiences with his dad and other authority figures, or if he unknowingly absorbed the lessons in life he was afforded. At what point did he begin to think about the usefulness of those exchanges, or did he even think about it at all? Much like golfers wandering down the first fairway, everything is in front of them. They don't always consciously record their early experiences, observations, and learnings to use later in the round. Basics like the weather, wind direction and ground condition might be taken in. As with a young person starting out in life, any observation a golfer makes on the first hole is predominantly external and objective. There is very little subjective self-awareness about the individual's state of mind, feelings, or effect on those around the person.

At what point in the round does their thinking change? And why does it change? How many times are the learnings from past rounds forgotten by the time the golfer steps up to the first tee again? Interestingly, changes always occur within the round. Why is that? The most prominent changes are almost always related to mood, attitudes, and temper rather than have anything to do with technique or skill. Curiously, the things we ignore at the beginning can overwhelm us later in the round and take on much more importance, just as they do in life.

Irrespective of whether Dave consciously or unconsciously learned these valuable lessons, he has applied them ever since in both his professional and personal interactions. He cleverly encourages you to find the answers to these and a thousand other questions so adroitly that you are rarely aware of it. It took me years to realise he was doing it in many areas of my life, not just on the golf course.

As we all did, Dave navigated his childhood and teenage years surrounded by an array of influences that helped shape his character and style, developing an emotional intelligence that was to be such a formidable feature of his caddying success. I have been reliably told by people close to him during his younger years that while fairly quiet, he exhibited a strength and maturity far beyond his age. He projected a considered thoughtfulness that often surprised people, catching them off guard when he vocalised his views. He had the aura of an "old soul" that now and then, you notice in someone. How does such a young man instinctively understand situations better than most and then remarkably have sensible suggestions and solutions to offer? It happened so frequently that everyone around him used to say, "That's just our Davey." I still notice that knowing sparkle behind his eyes. It's as if he has experienced most situations before, and I find myself relying on that insight more than I care to admit. Strangely, it is comforting.

To illustrate my point about how attitudes can change from the first couple of holes to later in the round, I'd like to share a personal experience. Davey was caddying for me in the club championships. We started out just as I outlined earlier. All the players were positive, enthusiastic, and relatively upbeat. On the first hole, one of my opponents hit his ball into a questionable lie in the hazard behind a tree. He was fairly relaxed and was even happy to take advice from the rest of us on where he could take a drop. Dave was his usual pragmatic self and offered the best interpretation of the rule. His suggestion was accepted, and the player duly took the drop and managed a respectable bogey.

Later in the round on the 15th hole, the same player, who

had been experiencing one of those rounds we all dread, found himself in a similar position, this time only worse. Instead of doing exactly as he did on the 1st hole, taking a drop and limiting the damage, he decided out of desperation to try a miracle shot and of course it didn't come off, and he hit it deeper in the hazard. Well, this player's head came right off; he went berserk, attacking the offending tree with his club and the sound of the ferocious impacts only equalled by the furious cursing and yelling. Dave summed up the situation in an instant and said,

"Looks like Steve is doing a little course renovation work. The greens committee have wanted to chop that tree down for ages. He's always been very helpful like that."

Well, we all broke up; even Steve, who after having a good laugh at his loss of control, recovered to make a double bogey and then managed to par the last three holes. A classic example of how our state of mind at separate times can produce a starkly different reaction in precisely the same situation. It also demonstrates super caddy in action!

Wouldn't it be useful if we could maintain the positive expectations and enthusiasm we have at the start of a round throughout the whole day? Being in that state allows us to be less afraid of mistakes and apply clear-headed thinking to decisions, and even if something goes wrong, we don't stress too hard early in the round. Just like Steve, later in the round, we can easily end up in a very different mental state.

Either you are frustrated and angry because you have played poorly, or you have had a series of unlucky incidents. Both can cause you to give up and play recklessly and start hitting low percentage shots. If you are playing well, you begin to stress about preserving your round, and you start to protect your score and play conservatively to avoid mistakes, which is precisely the opposite of what is needed. You didn't get to a good position by playing cautiously. We've all done it, so in both these situations why do we change our strategy?

We have all heard it said that you play your best golf when you play like you don't care. But there is more to it than that. If you played without caring you would not focus or prepare properly for each shot; you wouldn't aim accurately; you would blaze away and be cavalier. That's not how you achieve your best performance. I believe what people mean when they say that, is they play without fear. By that, I mean playing without the fear of the outcome, the fear of ruining a good score, the fear of looking bad, or the fear of bad breaks. People often say that they were hitting it great on the practice range but once out on the course, it went pear-shaped and they started to hit shots that they never would hit on the range. What has changed? It's the same person with the same skill level, the same physiology on the day, and the same equipment. The only thing that has changed is the pressure of the situation and the change of your mental state.

I think it's also to do with time and motion. There is so

much time in golf when you are not actually playing a shot. If the average golfer hits 85 shots in a round and the time it takes to hit each shot, not preparing for the shot but actually hitting the ball, is around 2 secs, then in a four and a half hour round you only spend 170 secs playing shots, less than 3 minutes. That means just 1.1% of your time on the course is actually spent physically playing golf. The rest of the time is free for mental meandering. On the practice range, you are continually hitting shots.

Then there is motion. In most other sports the ball and the opposing players are moving, and you respond to what they and the ball are doing. You develop your skills at practice and during a game you instinctively react to the movement of the ball and the other players. In golf, the ball is still. Your mental state affects how you play more than most other sports, and you have more time to think in between shots than any other sport, no wonder it is so hard. That is why in other sports the range between your best performances and your worst performances is much less than in golf. In this game, your worst golf can be atrocious and yet your best performances are right at the other end of the scale. Throw in the variables such as the endless variety of shots compared to other sports, and it only adds to the complexity. Remember every shot in golf has infinite lengths, elevations, and wind, turf, and sand conditions, whereas while most sports might have their own particular variables, they have a finite sized court or field. When you serve in tennis, it is the same length court and the same net height every single time. In cricket, the length of the pitch and the size of the stumps never change. In Baseball the diamond and the distance between bases have official dimensions; the distance the pitcher throws the ball is always consistent. Similarly, in Basketball, the size of the court and the zones don't change. The net and backboard are always the same height and size. You can practice a free throw, a pitch, a serve, or a ball in cricket reliably because you know the precise length it will be in a game. In a round of golf, you rarely hit two shots the same distance or height.

So golf is a difficult and variable game where the players are prone to letting their mental state affect their performance, and there is way too much time to think about all of the variables, so what do we do? What can a caddy do to help?

Just as we find in our day to day lives, there is no easy fix, no simple prescription but there are ways to change your mental approach over time that can help you become a better golfer and a nicer person living a happier life.

2ND HOLE

Once on the second hole, you begin to consider the early stages of responsibility. You think about the things you should be focusing on, and evaluate what is important, and you sense a vague recognition of what is expected of you. You're still relatively carefree enough that there isn't any perceptible change in your behaviour externally, but you feel it inside. We sense similar things in our early adulthood. Think about how you felt when you were 18 or 20. You had left school and were starting to think about life differently, even if it was only from the frame of reference of your own particular environment and influences. You didn't really know what you would do, or could do, but the pressures of what you should do were starting to build and be noticeable.

Davey was just like the rest of us as a young adult. He had some idea of what his future might be but wasn't entirely certain what it would look like or how he would get there. His entry into professional golf as a caddy was quite unexpected and unplanned enough to be described as accidental, but that was a little later. At this stage of his life, a career in the arts or entertainment was his first interest. He was a naturally talented artist and photographer, and he did some study to support this, but he ended up working in the busy and burgeoning film, TV and music industry. He worked in audio recording, camera operations, and overall production, a lot of it in the high-pressure environment of live broadcasting where he rose to technical director. Sport, music, film and TV production kept him busy and stimulated him for some years. In hindsight, spending so much time recording sounds and images and capturing moments in time may well have influenced his way of getting the best out of golfers and people around him later on his journey. He is very effective at remembering key points in time and past events to highlight an important message or to motivate the required actions and behaviours from others.

In the early days, one of the broadcasts he was working on was the Australian Open at The Australian Golf Club in Sydney. Dave didn't even play a lot of golf at this time, but at these first few tournaments, he began to feel quite a strong connection to golf developing, a feeling that was almost spiritual and the force of emotion surprised him. He still finds it hard to understand or explain today. Everything about this game felt familiar to him, and more importantly, it felt as if it was meant to be, more than just fate, it was supposed to happen, and there wasn't any point resisting the calling. Golf chose him.

He confided in me once, and I know he has only told one other person this story, that on the final morning of the tournament, he was out early, working alone as the sun was rising, laying out some extra cabling when he heard a voice behind him.

"Do you know why you are here?" Davey spun around annoyed at what he thought was a ridiculous question,

"Of course I know, and if the bloody delivery truck hadn't run over and broken our lines last night, I wouldn't be out here at all."

There was no one there. But as he squinted through the low sun on the horizon he could see a golfer and his caddy industriously at work on the practice range. As he focused he suddenly realised it was Jack Nicklaus and his caddy. The best golfer of all time, the major drawcard for this event, a player who wasn't due to tee off for about 6 hours was grinding hard on the range and appeared to be listening intently to every word from the caddy. Dave couldn't resist getting a little closer, and he noticed that the caddy would go out about 110 metres with his shag bag in his hand.

Remember this was the time when even the greatest players of the day had to bring their own practice balls. Jack would hit a series of shots, and the caddy would catch them on the first bounce in the bag and then bring them back, each time with some serious feedback. Then they would start over. Dave was astounded when he heard Jack ask the caddy,

"Which way are they spinning after they land? Left or right?" Now Jack was never known for his wedge game, perhaps because the rest of his game was at such a high level that by comparison, his wedge play looked mortal. The fact was this week he had a hit some poor wedges, and he was now 4 shots back from the leader in the final round. What the caddy said next is permanently engraved in Dave's memory.

"Remember the last hole at Pebble Beach 8 years ago when you spun it left down that slight slope to 12 inches?"

"Yes!" Jack curtly answered.

"Do you also remember the smell of the ocean that day?" Jack was quiet for a few seconds, and then he said,

"Actually I do, and I also remember the music playing in one of the houses on that hole and the aroma of the BBQ they were cooking wafting across the 18th". The caddy purposefully waited until Jack looked up at him.

"Well you made an adjustment that morning that helped you hit that same shot three times in the round, that's what we need to find today."

Jack's mind and his muscle memory instantly went back eight years, and he quickly went to work. He wanted to finish practising before the other golfers reached the range and saw what he was working on, but he also fully intended to let them see him leaving and get them wondering why he was out there so early. Even those who didn't see him would soon hear about it. They weren't going to be in his mind at all during the round but he was definitely going to be in theirs. Nearby, someone else was also leaving in a hurry.

Dave headed back to the TV trailer, he was running late now, but he kept thinking about this exchange all day, especially when Jack birdied the last hole to shoot 65 and win the tournament, in part thanks to some sharp wedge play. What struck Dave the most was here was the great Jack Nicklaus out at dawn working hard to find a shot he needed, and his caddy used an old memory to help him get it. Then he recalled that mysterious voice and he realised why he was meant to be there…

We all have moments like that in our lives, lots of them. Pivotal, transformative instants that can be as simple as a chance encounter with someone where one comment can get us thinking or even change the way we think, or a stunning awakening when we discover a fundamental truth or our real purpose in life is revealed to us. Large or small, these instances are all points of inflexion that may either give us options about the course we take, or at other times circumstances and situations are thrust upon us and we must deal with the consequences, but in every case there is change. This day was of the former variety for Dave, he had experienced a revelation and he had to make some decisions…

An interesting question is raised in the Jack Nicklaus story. Why did the greatest golfer in history need to be helped to remember how to play a shot he has probably played thousands of times? And how did a seemingly insignificant recollection trigger the memory and find the solution? There is a school of thought that we can pass on or even influence the behaviour of others with our emotions. If someone smiles, you tend to smile as well. If they frown, chances are you will. If someone falls or hurts themselves, you probably will wince. The body language of others and their projected emotion can influence how we feel and perhaps even how we act. Jack's caddy shared a powerful memory using the sense of smell; Jack then enhanced it with a sound he also remembered and another aroma, the BBQ. The caddy recalled his memory, synchronised it with Jack's recollection, shared the feelings and linked it to a successful outcome, and most importantly called up the mechanics of how to do it from the mental filing cabinet, to apply eight years later.

Dave has used that approach with me countless times,

"Remember the day you made a birdie from this fairway bunker?" Immediately I am back there.

"Last summer, straight after that break we had for a

thunderstorm, you came back out and hit a low running cut shot around one tree and under the next and ran it up to 10 feet. You've got that shot, let's see it again."

What amazes me most is how he can get me to play shots almost at will. Even on days when I am playing poorly and have no feel, he will describe where he wants me to hit it, remind me of when I've done it before and miraculously, most times I can do it. It's like he gives me permission to make the shot, I need him in my ear when he is I can do remarkable things. I am sure that is why he has been such a success on tour. If he can get results with his friend in an amateur club competition, what is possible with a world-class professional golfer?

Who is in your ear? Both on the course and off it, how do you store, recall and use the feelings associated with the memories of past performances at precisely the moment when you need them most? All of us, including those at the top of their sport or vocation, tend to forget how to do this, much less understand how it works and why it is so useful. We all need a super caddy at our shoulder whispering in our ear.

After that day in Sydney Dave continually thought about what had happened. The strange voice he was certain he had heard, what he had witnessed between Nicklaus and his caddy and the unexpected but inspiring emotional impact all of it had on him. He found himself dreaming about becoming knowledgeable enough to be a caddy on tour, and he imagined how much satisfaction he would feel if he was able to contribute to the success of his player. Most of all he was intrigued by the power of communication and the psychology of performance. However, the clash of his sense of responsibility and the allure of his dreams was a growing internal conflict, tormenting him. Dave knew he needed to decide and so he reasoned that it was appropriate he should apply the same approach he believed a good caddy would use to lead his player to the right decision. That is be clear on the objective, look at the options for reaching the goal, analyse the risks and once the decision is made commit to it fully.

Dave started to study golf, and he read everything he could about the game and its history. He was enthralled by the stories about the great champions and how in the crucial moments when even under enormous pressure they were still able to perform and achieve amazing results. More and more it became clear to him that the thought processes employed by the player were more critical to the outcome than the technical applications of the golf swing. The control and utilisation of their emotions and state of mind often gave the top players that tiny edge they needed over the other players. You see it all the time on tour, once a player wins, particularly if it is a major championship, then they tend to win more often or at the very least be in contention more. All that has changed is their self-belief has increased, and they feel they belong at that level. They have learned how to play

it occurred or when it might happen again. Dave believed that we all should be able to do it on demand, although he had no idea how to actually achieve this at the time, so he began his research. He knew he had the ability to observe people and situations and make sense of what was happening and could see solutions quicker than most people. These skills could be put to good use. So he resolved the best way to observe golfers and monitor how they think was to be around them. Dave began to play golf regularly. Given his aptitude for ball sports like AFL and cricket, he soon became a good player and yet even as he had some success, and his handicap quickly dropped to a low single marker, he never changed his objective. Playing golf was an enjoyment, but for him it was always his course of study, his professional development. The golf course was his classroom, and it was a rich source of material. He always said that if you want to learn something about people, even those you believe you know well; spend some regular time with them on the golf course. Personality, ethics and values, honesty, sportsmanship, how people respond to pressure, what fear does to them, how competitive they can be it's all revealed on the golf course!

Dave was relatively guarded with his privacy and still is. As his mum often resignedly says,

"He is an unknown quantity."

This feature of his personality helped keep his ambitions

secret from his family and circle of friends for quite some time. Even when Dave made changes such as taking up golf or travelling around the country to tournaments as a spectator because he rarely confided to anyone his deepest thoughts and feelings, nobody thought much of these changes or bothered to question him because they had learned that he wouldn't give a complete answer anyway. It was probably good that he didn't share his dreams at this stage because he would have inevitably been criticised and discouraged by well-meaning family and mates. Predictably they would have reminded him of his responsibilities and lectured him about the right way to live and implored him to develop a career, start a family and have an accepted type of life, especially in the context of his country town upbringing. But for Dave this meant an unexceptional life, so for a long time, he kept it all to himself.

The choice Dave made to keep his ambitions and plans secret from his loved ones to avoid the predictable reactions reminds me of my great uncle, Doug Nanfield. He quietly went away and enlisted in the army in World War II; somehow he got in even though he was a few months too young and ended up serving in the Asia region. He knew the family would have disapproved and then tried to stop him from going, so he didn't let them know. He distinguished himself through his bravery and the way he encouraged and supported the other men in his unit. Ultimately, he was captured by the Japanese and died in captivity. My grandmother never recovered from the loss of her beloved brother and spent her whole life carrying around a painful mixture of anger and heartbreak. When I was born nearly twenty years after he died, my parents named me after him. For my father there was never going to be any other choice of a name.

3RD HOLE

Around the third hole in a round, the noise levels start to change. The banter reduces in intensity and is less light-hearted. The players focus a little harder and contemplate what has happened so far and what they need to do. A good start carries the weight of making sure we don't waste it, and a poor start creates the pressure of playing catch up. Expectations may rise, or a resignation might creep into the player's mindset that it could be a difficult day. You feel something similar when you are in your early 20's. You are still optimistic because there is so much of life in front of you, but it's hard not to evaluate your progress so far and pose questions to yourself. "Am I on track? Am I making the right choices? Have I wasted any opportunities? What should I improve? Do I need to make any changes? How do I look to those around me?

One thing that Dave noticed very early in his study of golfers was there was commonly a universal reset after nine holes. Nearly all the people he played with were able to reset their mental state after nine holes as if it was a brand new round. He even experienced it himself. No matter how poorly the first nine has been played, or what catastrophic disasters and bad luck they had endured, players would look forward to the second nine with heightened positivity and put the recent past behind them.

"It's a new nine now." "Let's have a good back side," they would encouragingly say to each other. Interestingly the mood and banter would also lift and in many cases, people would play better on the back nine. What has changed except the mental state? Conversely, if a player had scored well on the front nine often the reset didn't happen, and the pressure kept on building. It occurred to Dave that if it could happen every 3 holes instead of after nine that it would be a much better way to play. A series of six separate games of three holes had to be more manageable physically and mentally. Navigating a much shorter period in which to maintain your composure and deal with the pressure must help performances. Wouldn't it be beneficial to experience that fresh start mentality 6 times in a round? Dave had even considered approaching the club to change the scorecards to format them into 6 sections of three holes to help players achieve the change of attitude. He figured that the nine-hole phenomena had only developed because people sometimes just play nine holes, the scorecards are traditionally organised into two nines and scoring, countbacks and even betting are in 9 hole groupings. He made a note to employ this approach with his players once he began caddying.

The notion of applying the 3 hole segmentation idea to our lives has merit to. If we could reset our emotions, mental approach, motivation, and our behaviours into shorter periods using realistic targets, would that help us be more effective in our relationships, our jobs, hobbies, interests, health, and cope better with the challenges we all must face at times? Would we be more optimistic and fresher? Would it help attenuate long-term stress? We all use various forms of a to-do list. If we use shorter listings and can tick off many of the items as soon as possible, it gives us a sense of control and achievement. If we just keep adding to the long list and aren't finishing many of the things on the list, the stress builds, and we feel more and more out of control. Nothing is more paralysing than living without hope, feeling and believing that you just can't get the result you desire. If you can see the target, you have a greater chance of hitting it. If you can visualise the shot and believe you can make it, magic can happen.

The only expectations you should live up to are your own. Davey instinctively knew this was a fundamental truth. No matter how thorough the preparation, or how well the caddy and the support team get their golfer to the right place mentally and physically, it is the player who must hit the shot in the key moment.

Many years ago Dave was teaching his younger sister to ride a bike, he did all the usual things, giving the basic instructions, holding onto the back of the bike while she got the feel of it, running alongside and stopping her from falling. They weren't making much progress; she was so afraid of coming off the bike and didn't believe that she would ever learn and was embarrassed because the neighbours were watching the entertainment.

"Don't let go of me Davey!" she would squeal. For a while, he didn't let go, but then a realisation came to him. If he continued to be her safety net, she could never develop the belief required.

"Livvy I am going to let go, and you might fall a couple of times, but I promise you I will be here to pick you up. When Dad taught me, I fell off a dozen times. How good will you feel when you do it by falling off fewer times than I did? Wouldn't you like to beat me?"

"You bet I do" she shot back with determination. Dave was 13 when this happened, and his maturity and approach was impressive for his age. It was a similar technique to the one he has used innumerable times since on the golf course. He described the situation, identified the target, helped his sister visualise the outcomes and set a challenge and asked for commitment while making sure that she knew the responsibility was hers alone. His sister Olivia, or Livvy as he affectionately calls her, was riding unaided after only seven tumbles off the bike. The image of the beaming proud smile on her beautiful young face, shining through the dust and the tear tracks touches his heart to this day.

Everyone is aware of the importance of managing expectations, but it is not that easy to do especially on your own. As soon as you begin to think about the responsibility of doing so you are creating another one. It becomes circular; you have the added expectation that you should be able to manage your expectations. Dave intuitively recognised this conundrum. He realised that it is vital to "disengage the stress" of the moment. To help people get out of their own way he would distract them enough to relieve the pressure but still retain the underlying intent in their subconscious. We all have the amazing ability to do that. Consider how we can drive a car, throw a ball or ride a bike without thinking too hard about the mechanics. In fact, we do it better when we don't consciously focus on the technique. Once we have learned the skill, it is more effective if we just let it happen. The pressure of the situation can do funny things to our mind and subsequently our performance. Think about the often used example of how easily you can walk across a plank that is six inches off the ground compared to if it were a thousand feet in the air.

Dave used his "disengage the stress" technique perfectly on me when we played together in the Foursomes Match Play championships a few years ago. I was playing badly at the time, and that morning on the practice range I was hitting it terribly. It felt like I was in someone else's body and my confidence was rock bottom. It is even worse in foursomes because you have the added pressure of not letting your partner down in the alternate shot format. Dave could sense my state of mind as we walked to the first tee. Normally I would hit the opening tee shot but he offered to take it that day, and I was a little relieved when he did and more so when he hit it straight down the fairway. What he did next was as beautifully simple as it was clever. All the way down that fairway as we approached the ball Dave engaged me in a conversation about the best way to cook scallops. Dave and I both enjoyed food and cooking and often discussed recipes and methods. The night before at a dinner party with friends and partners, Dave had made his signature dish, scallops, and burnt butter sauce. Suddenly I was focused on cooking technique and not stressing about the consequences of hitting a poor shot and putting Dave in trouble for the next one. Our opponents looked across at us as if we were crazy. As I hit my shot from the fairway, I'm sure I was still talking about how much brown sugar he used in the sauce as I started the backswing. I hit that 8 iron as pure as I have ever done in my life, the ball never left the flag and it

his research; he was making changes to his routines and his lifestyle and continuously evaluating his progress. Still, there was nagging doubt in his mind, and he was worried about how those closest to him would regard it. He was a little puzzled about why this was such an issue. He had always been his own man, self-reliant, strong-minded, and he thought, not that concerned about how others viewed him. So why couldn't he get past this and be comfortable with this choice of career and life path? He thought about this for weeks and the only conclusion reached so far was that he knew he must find a resolution to this problem because it would hold him back if he couldn't. He was reasonably sure that his family, just like most people, primarily want their children and siblings to be happy and fulfilled and achieve enough success to live the life they desire and to do it in a manner that enriched other people's lives without causing any harm. If he became a successful caddy wouldn't he meet these aspirations? Of course, so why was he troubled about his choice? Why hadn't he told anyone yet?

He was lying in bed early one morning rolling it around in his head once more when the comprehension hit him so suddenly it jolted him upright out of that place between sleep and wakefulness. It was his issue, deep down he was worried about the stigma of being a caddy, working as an assistant to someone else, or maybe even being seen as a servant. It was his hang-up no one else's. As quickly as this realisation hit him, the solution rapidly followed. He loved all the aspects of being a caddy, helping, advising, leading, coaching and motivating. It was definitely not a role based on servitude. As soon as he framed the position in his mind as one of a guide, a mentor providing counsel and direction, a psychologist, manager and supporter then the problem vanished forever. Dave dialled a number; he hoped his dad was up this early, he had some news to tell him…

As the phone rang, he drifted back a few years to a chat he had with his Dad about why he chose to become a plasterer and a builder. His grandfather was a dairy farmer, and his dad had worked the farm as well as a young lad, and it would have been expected that he would continue in that type of work. Despite working extraordinarily hard on the farm, there wasn't any real satisfaction apart from helping out the family, so Dave's father decided to have a break and travel around Australia by motorbike. On this adventure, he saw and experienced more in those 12 months than he had done in all his prior years. He always said he grew up quickly on that trip and when he returned he took a job in a timber mill, learning all aspects of the business. Whilst there he befriended the owners of a plastering company and they offered to teach him the trade. He learned fast and was a highly valued employee but once again he wanted to be in control of his own destiny and he felt he could do better working for himself and so he started his own business.

People thought he was mad taking such a risk in those times and leaving a steady job but much like Dave does, he felt strongly about his calling. Dave recalled what his Dad said during one of the conversations they had about his past that now had such a weighty relevance.

"Dave your happiness is your own responsibility, only your choices and your actions will bring you true happiness. No one else has accountability for your happiness or authority over it. So do what makes you happy, not what other people expect you to do, and believe in it."

Back then Dave thought his dad might have been merely justifying his life choices, but now in retrospect, he saw the profound wisdom in his father's words. It sounds simple but taking your own initiative, especially when it concerns your dreams and goals can be challenging, especially if you detour off the traditional or accepted path. If you don't fully commit, you risk being tentative and not fully engaged, and the result will reflect the level of effort. Golfers experience this all the time. If you aren't committed and confident about the shot you have chosen to make, then your execution and result will reflect the lack of belief.

4TH HOLE

By the 4th hole, you usually have realised what you have physically that day, and you will need to work with whatever you've got. Different parts of your game may or may not be working well, and you need to recognise it and factor that into your game plan and your shot choices. How you navigate the challenges and take advantage of the opportunities is influenced by the tools you have on the day. Much like life, when everything is going well and coming together easily it's possible to cruise on auto pilot. However, if you're continually in cruise mode, you don't learn as much or develop the same skills and attributes that you do when you are battling through setbacks and challenges. Curiously we all seem to begin to run into these headwinds in our mid-twenties. What we learn about ourselves and how we make use of that knowledge is the real prize.

"**A**re there any local members around today who know this course well? My caddy has been delayed. Apparently, there's been an accident on the Bruce Highway, and the road is blocked both ways, he won't be able to get here for hours."

Rod Hazelbrook was one of the marquee young players playing in the pro-am at Pelican Waters Golf Club on Queensland's Sunshine Coast. He had sought out Dave for help. As a member of the organising committee, Dave had been involved in the planning of this event for the last six months. It had been a lot of hard work, but now that the tournament had started there wasn't much left to attend to, and the plan was to go out and enjoy watching the golf. Yes there would be any number of members who would jump at the chance to caddy for Rod Hazelbrook but would they do as good a job as Dave? For a brief instant, his natural tendency to not put his own interests first caused a momentary hesitation. Then with a clear-headed certainty, he saw this as one of those opportunities that are presented to us rarely, and if we don't grab them with conviction, they are lost forever.

When I hear people on the course rationalising after a bad hole by saying "that's ok you can get it back with a birdie or two" I always think to myself no you can't. I understand the sentiment of the encouragement, and it is important to focus and try to make the best score that you can despite the mistake. However, those shots can never be retrieved they are gone forever. So is a missed opportunity and Dave was not going to let this one slip by without at least trying to take it.

"I'd be more than happy to help you out Rod, where's your bag we're on the tee in 15 mins." Dave's confident response neatly solved Rod's problem and put him at ease.

If golf was easy, it would be boring after a while. Golfers continually moan about the difficulty of the game and the unfairness of the bad bounces and the unlucky lies, but if it wasn't such a challenge, and a lifelong quest for perfection then after a month or two you would be looking for something else to play. Everyone would be off scratch, making a hole in one each week, and there would be little reward for practising hard and applying the right emotional and strategic mindset. It's the highs and lows and specifically the distance between them that make this game so seductive and addictive. Desiring something that you cannot easily or frequently attain is a considerably more powerful motivation than if you can have whatever you want anytime you want it. Hitting the perfectly thought out and executed shot is a rare and wondrous experience, and the frequency of that experience is inversely proportionate to the size of your handicap. The rarity increases the intensity of the feeling. It's intoxicating.

Dave enjoyed the whole experience of caddying for Rod that afternoon. Seeing a top level player and how he approaches the game and applies his craft was incredibly educational although Dave still identified some areas where a slight change of mindset might help. One observation surprised Dave. A highly skilled player has to deal with an added complexity to shot selection that an amateur doesn't. They have a vast repertoire of shots at their disposal and such a high degree of confidence in their ability to hit any shot with precise control of flight that selecting the most appropriate one can be harder. Additional factors like ego, expectations, and their position on the leaderboard and the resultant state of mind widens the choices. Plus of course how they were feeling physically that day and which shots were working better on the range before they started. Most amateurs have their stock shot shape and struggle to move the ball either way or hit it lower or higher on demand, and can rarely hold it up into a cross breeze and they most certainly don't think about spinning it left or right as Jack Nicklaus was. Pros can also hit the same club a wide range of distances if required, something else that amateurs don't do that well. A top professional can be walking up to their ball with 8 or 10 shot choices in mind. The caddy's role Dave reasoned was critical both in the provision of all the information needed to reach the correct decision and then helping the pro through the decision making process positively to get them fully committed to the plan and confident about the outcome.

That's a lot to accomplish in a couple of minutes, particularly under the pressure of tournament conditions.

Superior capability doesn't always make it any easier. Dave used to say "proficiency doesn't always equal efficiency." Just because you're good at something doesn't mean you will perform at an optimum level, it is often the opposite. It's not how you perform compared to everyone else that matters; it is how you perform compared to your own potential. Another concept of Dave's is the "elasticity of ability." It basically means how far you can stretch your talent and what are the causes and effects? I believe that the gift of talent is not given randomly and it should not be wasted. There is a duty to fulfil the promise. I do not know why some people are blessed with high functioning skills and others aren't. Whether it is music, art, sport, literature, science, business, drama, medicine, people skills or any discipline from an infinite list, there are always those who are bestowed with astonishing skill and talent. Who really knows where that comes from but those that have it still only do so for a short time; they have the responsibility of stewardship for that ability during that period. While not many of us may be world class we all have capabilities to some degree, and we share a similar responsibility, if only to ourselves. How are you recognising, nurturing and managing your own talents?

That afternoon Dave developed a deeper appreciation of the role of the caddy and it only made him more determined that this was what he was meant to do. He was also pleased and just a little proud that a number of times during the round Rod appeared to place his complete trust in Dave's knowledge of the course and the conditions and would accept without challenge a suggestion. At first, he thought it might just be how a professional naturally separates the roles between player and caddy. His job is to play the shots and the caddy has to provide accurate data and make sensible suggestions. There is no doubt some truth to that, but more than once he asked for Dave's input and thanked him genuinely when the shot was successful and he would have stopped doing that if Dave was doing a poor job. Clearly, he didn't feel that way, and they made a good connection because within 12 months Dave was on his bag full time. Rod didn't win the pro-am that day, but to Dave, it is one of his own fondest career achievements because it was the start of it all.

Dave's caddying career began that day at Pelican Waters. Indeed so many important events in my own life also had their origin at this golf course. I met Dave there many years ago when I first moved into the area. I went through a number of my own challenges during the next few years, as did Dave. Coincidently we both had some concurrent serious health issues, and marriage breakdowns and helping each other work through the difficult periods only strengthened the friendship. No matter what we were dealing with, golf was the reassuring constant. It gave us a topic to discuss, something to look forward to, and an escape from the constrictions of our problems. This glorious game is much more than a distraction though; it is a portal to an uplifting place where the human spirit can be reinvigorated.

The most important occasion, however, was meeting Dave's sister. Olivia had been through her own ups and downs, and she had moved closer to Dave to help him through an especially tough time. I was doing my best to keep his spirits up but wasn't in the same class as her when it came to providing emotional support. The ever-present, unconditional help and the selfless assistance of his gentle, loving sister was an honour even to witness. I have always called her my angel, but she is most definitely Dave's angel as well. In the same dining room at the club where all that time ago Dave had offered to caddy for Rod Hazelbrook and kick-started his caddying career, I attended a Melbourne cup function and couldn't believe my good fortune when I walked in, and there was an empty seat next to Olivia, my future wife. Well at the time I thought it was just luck, later on, I learned the truth; the deft planning skills of super caddy were in play that day. I had arranged to meet Dave there, and when I got there, I assumed I had arrived before he had. In fact, I discovered years later that not only had he harangued a less than enthusiastic Olivia to attend, but he was already there before I was and had spent twenty minutes hiding around the corner of the bar and firmly but good-naturedly shepherding away anyone who tried to sit in the seat next to his sister. Then afterward he casually invited both of us to his place for dinner after the function. I remember thinking on the night why was he so prepared, and why was the table already set for three when we got to his place? He had been moving the chess pieces around for some time. Over about a 6 month timeframe I would often get an invite from Dave to attend a dinner or a party and Olivia just happened to be there as well. He would arrange for her to give me a lift somewhere or ask me to help her with some planning ideas for her new business. I guess I was a little slow to pick up the signals.

A year later I proposed to her at a single white linen covered table set beautifully for morning tea by the catering staff in the garden outside of the clubhouse. My soon to be brother in law was waiting nearby in a limousine to take us to a celebratory lunch. As always he was clearing the paths and charting the course. We just needed to trust and follow his directions.

5TH HOLE

Amateur golfers nearly always approach each game with the hopeful expectation they might play to the absolute peak of their ability. Their mindset on each shot early in their round visualises and recalls the best shot they have ever played from a similar position, especially on a familiar course. These moments are rare and unlikely to be repeated that often, so the most common emotions they then experience are disappointment and frustration, particularly if they use a strategy and a club choice consistent with their infrequent pure strikes. The realisation that hits them after a few holes can produce a dejected player in a depressed state. In life, we have all experienced the sobering shock when we discover someone who we have admired and looked up to isn't perfect. The halo effect we have applied to them evaporates, and it saddens us.

However, if we accept the reality that nobody is perfect and everyone has flaws, it can heighten the appreciation of their skills and high points and attenuate the disappointment. Adjust the expectation, and you can manage the weaknesses without surprise and then joyfully celebrate the successes.

D ave had experienced an unusually restless night. The anticipation of caddying for Rod at a major European event, The Irish Open, being played at a course acknowledged by many as one of the greatest in the world, Ballybunion, was more than enough to get anyone keyed up. However, from the moment he saw the draw for the first two rounds he couldn't sit still. They were playing with Seve Ballesteros! From the time Dave had started to study the history of golf, devouring everything he could in print and on film of the great players and moments in the game, his admiration for the legendary Spaniard had continually grown. Now he would have the enormous privilege of seeing him close up in competition. Rod had played with him before, and when Dave expressed how much this meant to him, Rod said with a wry smile,

"Don't get too excited Davey, he's an interesting character." Dave had, of course, read about the gamesmanship and moodiness but put that down to Seve's fierce competitiveness and relentless determination. Here was a chance to see a pure genius at work. In his expectant state, Dave missed the warning in Rod's typical Aussie understatement.

Despite not sleeping well, Dave couldn't wait to get to the range; he collected Rod's clubs and bounced down the path. Rod was chatting to a couple of friends from the tour; Dave went ahead and found a spot on the range. He was tempted to set up near Seve who he had noticed straight away at the far end of the practice area but decided not to appear too eager. He would have all day to observe him, besides the atmosphere between him and his caddy seemed a little tense. Even from 15 metres away Dave could feel the energy swirling around Seve, a stored, latent power so palpable he expected to air to start crackling like a high school science experiment. His swing still looked as languid and powerful as Dave had seen in old videos and the crowd five deep behind him looked on in appreciative awe, but the man himself was not pleased. He was muttering to himself, alternating between Spanish and shorthand English. Something was bothering him about the balls, and so he sent his caddy off to get a different bucket which didn't seem to help much. Then he sat on a chair and relaced his right shoe three or four times. All of this absorbed Dave, and he didn't see or hear Rod walk up behind him.

"We could move a little closer if you'd like Dave?" Rod whispered about a foot behind him. Startled, Dave nearly dropped the clubs he had in his

"Is he always this edgy Rod?" Dave asked without shifting his gaze from Seve.

"Oh no, normally he is much more intense, come on let's get started."

As Rod worked through his usual methodical practice routine, Dave was wondering how Seve could play at the level he has for so long while appearing to work in an agitated state of mind? So many times in his stunning career he demonstrated inspiring brilliance unmatched by anyone and with the poise to be able to perform in the most pressurised situations this game can present. Dave realised his understanding about being in the zone and how to get into it was underdeveloped and needed refinement and expansion. Severiano Ballesteros was about to give him both. He caught a glimpse of it passing the chipping green area. Seve had stalked off the range almost in frustrated disgust and moved to spend a few final minutes on his short game. Dave didn't break his stride as he was hurrying to the putting green with Rod before they teed off, but he still was able to notice a significant change in Seve from what he had observed on the range. There was almost a soft glow around him, and despite hitting these gorgeous little flop shots over a bunker repeatedly stopping a couple of feet from the flag, he appeared to be doing it without even thinking or concentrating. His body language and facial expressions were entirely different to a few minutes ago. That incandescent smile of his was back lighting up the whole area. The short game was Seve's comfort zone, where his genius was undeniable. He knew he was the best at this part of the game, and so did everyone else. Nobody has ever had the imagination, feel and touch that he possessed. There are many jokes about God playing golf; perhaps he already did, through Seve's hands. People were consistently amazed at how often Seve could create a shot and escape from challenging places. They would marvel at how he could do it under such pressure. But Dave was beginning to realise there wasn't any pressure for him in these situations. This was where he felt comfortable, this was what he enjoyed doing, and Seve was relaxed because he knew he could do it; he had complete faith in his short game ability. If you have a look at him in pictures on the tee compared to when he is playing around the greens, you can see the difference. On the tee he looks under strain, he looks tense as if he is going into battle. Around the greens, he is serene and calm, like he is excited by the challenge. On the tee his eyes are dark with fierce determination as if he's facing an enemy; around the green, his eyes dance with eager anticipation, he is in his safe place.

So, Dave thought, the "zone" can be compartmentalised into segments of the game not just periods of time. Understanding how to achieve this was incredibly important, he needed to study some more. As he walked to the first tee with Rod, he smiled to himself, Professor Ballesteros's class was about to start.

The state of mind that everyone seeks which will help them effortlessly perform under pressure, commonly called the zone, is elusive. It's hard to get into that state, but when you achieve that feeling, it is very familiar and easily recognisable. Everything is comfortable, relaxed, time slows down, and the decision making and execution just flow. Distractions dissipate, and noises and movement go unnoticed.

Players will often say that they haven't ever experienced being in the zone. I would argue that we all have been in a mental state that approximates the feeling of being in the zone. Perhaps with varying degrees of intensity and milder levels of importance attached to the setting than others, but we have all been there. For example, everyone has certain holes they invariably play well. Unfortunately, we also have those holes we frequently play poorly but let's stay on the positive for now. The holes we play well are the ones where we feel confident and comfortable. A calmness envelopes us as we walk onto the tee, stress levels are lower, our minds clearer and our swing free and smooth. We can visualise the shot and play it almost casually knowing that the result will nearly always be positive. Now part of the reason is that the memories and positive feelings from past successes help grow our confidence, and we play without fear as talked about earlier, but how and why did we start performing well on a particular hole to begin building our memory bank? Have you ever tried to trick your mind into believing you are on a different hole? You play the 5th hole well all the time, but the 17th is your nightmare, so on the 17th tee, you attempt to convince yourself you are on the 5th tee. It is extraordinarily hard to do this. It is next to impossible for most of us. The other typical example is when we play a new course blissfully unaware of where the trouble lies, especially on blind holes and we hit beautiful shots to difficult positions, and then when we walk over the hill and see the hazards, we are surprised and delighted at the result. You know from painful experience what happens the next time you play those holes now armed with the knowledge of where the trouble is, it's not something that can be unremembered. So when you are given the advice to imagine the water isn't there or not to think about the out of bounds down the right side of the hole, how achievable is the instruction from your well-meaning buddy? How can we clear our minds and find that desired state?

No golfer is given or attains every skill. All will have a weakness, some players may be more balanced and well-rounded as a player than others, but they will still have an element of their game that isn't at the standard of the rest of their skill set. The imperfection though creates a reflected beauty in the higher functioning parts and spotlights the examples of exceptional ability. The contrast between the perfect and the imperfect magnifies the best parts. Seve intuitively knew this. He didn't appear to fear the mistakes but instead looked like he was relaxed waiting for the moments of brilliance to show up. The lack of one skill can often highlight the possession of another one. Rightly or wrongly we see a similar phenomenon in everyday life. A person who is consistently caring, unselfish and generous frequently does so much for others that it can go unnoticed at times. Often it is expected or anticipated that they will always be there to help out. However, if someone who is self-absorbed and mostly ignorant about the needs of others surprisingly shows compassion and consideration, then the contrast with their normal behaviour puts their rare act of kindness into sharper focus and produces a higher level of appreciation. Conversely, if an inherently good individual does anything that is shameful or wrong then the shock factor amplifies the awareness and the perceived severity of the transgression, and sadly, the punishment. An incongruity we all allow to exist principally unquestioned.

After 8 holes Dave had mentally kept the following statistics on Seve's round so far.

- *Fairways hit*   -   **1**
- *Greens in regulation* -   **3**

- *Number of putts*   -   7 (1 two-putt, 5 one putts and he chipped in twice)
- *Score*   -   **4 under par**

By comparison, Rod had hit 6 fairways, 7 greens in regulation and was 1 under with 14 putts. As the group walked off the ninth tee, Dave was thinking hard about the incredible differences in both scoring and method between the two players when he heard someone near him say,

"Will you remember why you're seeing this?" Dave stopped and turned but couldn't be sure who said it. There were a lot of people swarming around the small tee area racing ahead for vantage spots; it could have been any of them. After Rod and Seve had both played their second shots to the green, Seve walked up beside him and whilst staring straight ahead at the green said to him in hushed low tones,

"They speak to you also Davey, no?"

"Who does?" He wasn't sure if he was more shocked at the meaning behind the words or the fact that Seve had even spoken to him. Apart from introductions on the first tee he hadn't said a word to either Rod or himself all day. He didn't answer Dave's question as he was off hurriedly to his ball on the edge of the green and was now in animated discussion with his caddy.

The rest of the round was more routine, and despite

showing a couple of glimpses of his incredible short game, Seve struggled a little and played the back nine in 1 over and finished with a three under 69. Rod was his steady self and also posted a 69. Dave heard no more mysterious voices, but as he was finishing up cleaning and packing Rod's gear for the next day and getting ready to leave, Seve once more surprised him. In his usual assertive manner, he came over to Dave after everyone else had left and sat down to give him some advice.

"Listen to me I will tell you what you must do. Do not be afraid, as a boy I was at first scared but then when I eventually understand the meaning, it inspires me and gives me strength and I believe I was chosen to do something special." Dave was touched by such an intimate and helpful gesture, a side of the man not often reported, and so he thanked him sincerely. But then almost reassuring to his legend, Seve couldn't leave it there, as he stood, his pride which was often criticised as arrogance reared up.

"I know why they choose me, but you, I do not know?" he said disdainfully. With a troubled expression on his face and a puzzled shrug of his broad shoulders, Seve turned and strode imperially out of the locker room. That last comment still gives Dave a chuckle when he thinks about it now.

6ᵀᴴ HOLE

As the first third of the round is ending a noticeable rhythm is displayed by the player, in their movements, their swing, and their mood. It might be a ragged, out of time, multi-paced and inconsistent pattern, or a smooth, pleasing and predictable cadence, but it is a rhythm that did not exist at the start either way. Differing modulations and timbres in music appeal to diverse musicians and audiences. Intriguingly, some people seek variety and respond better in an environment of change. The challenge invigorates them. Others prefer one style and limit their range. Golfers need to understand their optimum tempo and move back to it if they are out of beat. The rhythm and balance of our lives affect the clarity of our vision and ultimately our enjoyment and performance. As our thirties loom, it might be worth checking our own personal life metronome.

Dave spent his thirty-fourth birthday in South Korea. It wasn't however, in the exotic or romantic setting you may have imagined. He was huddled in a small room of the clubhouse of the Gapyeong Benest Golf Club in Gyeonggi-Do. The course was designed by Jack Nicklaus, but Davey was sure Jack didn't design the clubhouse. The room that was now housing about 35 caddies was a windowless box that was also dark and stifling as the power had gone out not long after the storm had smashed into the course two hours ago. Although not on the coast the course still felt the savagery of the typhoon despite the intensity weakening as it moved over the land mass. Dave sat there not being able to communicate with many of the other people in the room because just as he had observed on tour with the Korean players, the caddies, employees, and officials also showed a reluctance to learn to speak English. Curiously they could generally understand spoken English but weren't able to or didn't want to speak it themselves. In a crowded space, buffeted by the noise of alarmed voices in a language he couldn't understand, and sitting in the middle of a country he had never visited before, and at this moment he was sure would never do so again, surrounded by people, Dave felt isolated and alone.

The cultural differences here were more pronounced than anywhere else he had been. The dismissive way some of the officials and players treated the caddies was surprising and had shocked Dave from day one. Although he had seen the oddities of the travelling Korean player on tour, for example bringing their own food to tournaments and keeping very much to themselves socially, he hadn't expected to be treated like this. As he sat here in the darkness that was disrupted only by the glow of mobile phones and laptops, he recalled a friend who had worked in the liquor industry telling him stories of his trips to Korea. One anecdote that had stuck in his mind described how the local executives would work very long hours and then go out to a late dinner with international visitors from the respective liquor companies. Every person at the table had a bottle of spirits placed in front them and it was considered bad manners not to finish it during the dinner. Then afterward some of the men would visit late night establishments for further "entertainment." This happened night after night. The part of the story that stunned him most though was that no matter what time the husband returned home after an extended night of drinking, entertainment and whatever else, the wife would get up and wash her husband's feet before he crossed the threshold of the dwelling. As he remembered this Dave laughed out loud imagining the somewhat different response an Australian executive could expect to receive should he come home in a similar fashion. There may have been more cutting off of appendages than any soothing washing of them going on in Aussie households! Entertaining as it was Dave always doubted the truth to the story but now that he was here he wasn't so sure. There definitely was evidence of gender and class inequity, at least that's how he interpreted it. Being herded into this room tersely and unsympathetically by the tournament staff did little to change his opinion at the time. He felt like a prisoner but at least the lowly prisoner could expect some food and water. Since being put in here, they hadn't received anything. The storm seemed to have passed, and Dave was jack of the whole episode and rose to leave, even if he had to physically force his way into the main clubhouse he was prepared to do so. Just then the doors opened, and the caddies were able to file out. Dave felt an angry shudder of disappointment as part of him wanted to have the confrontation, especially after he noticed the players and officials comfortably enjoying table service and hot food.

What was he doing here anyway? The main reason being another caddy he knows offered him the bag of a Korean girl. His friend had hurt his knee and couldn't work for two weeks, so he sold the idea to Dave as an adventure and the chance to experience the women's tour for the first time. The more personal reason baffled Dave. He remembered feeling quite surprised that he had agreed to go. It was way out of his comfort zone.

Initially, despite the language barriers, he found working with the player quite pleasant. The difficulty was with the team around her, especially the father. He was incredibly demanding, not only of Dave but he was also tough on his daughter. She dutifully did whatever he dictated. Dave found it a struggle because the father seemingly had little golf knowledge but insisted on exercising his authority, especially in practice rounds. Dave had always used this time to do a lot of work on scoping the course and developing the game plan, and in this case, he needed to obtain a working knowledge of her game swiftly. However, out on the course the father insisted on being physically involved in the practice, presumably to demonstrate to everyone his importance. At times he would introduce some bizarre routines. For example, he would go out to specific positions on the fairway when Dave and the player were on the tee, and he would place sticks with reflective stickers in different places and on various lines from the tee. These stickers could be picked up by the laser rangefinder. The daughter would then ask Dave how far to my father's stick before she would hit a shot. The only problem was he rarely had the sticks on the right line, so Dave would be wanting her to try a shot on the correct line, maybe fading it off the bunker on the left and the father is hammering sticks in the ground like a deranged market gardener 30 metres to the right and 20 metres shorter on the other side of the fairway. Around the practice greens, it was worse because he had the advantage of proximity. He would bark orders relentlessly to his daughter about where to land chips and bunker shots and again he was mostly wrong. That this girl had achieved any success at all on tour was a testament to her natural ability. But then as Dave became aware that most of the players had similar family and management controls in place, and all of them constantly practiced from dawn to dusk, often on the wrong things and sometimes risking injury, he surmised that all the players had a common encumbrance. When Dave tried to offer his view to the father or the manager, he was rudely interrupted and told not to speak. Dave felt rebuked like he was an insignificant slave. It made sense to him now why so many Asian and particularly Korean players, especially women, blossomed and improved when they went to the US and European tours. Their families often couldn't be out on tour all the time, so they had fewer restrictions and more freedom to work on the correct elements of their game and maximise the utility of their practice sessions. Plus the change in their state of mind would have been a significant relief for them.

Given how vital the realisation was for him that the role of a caddy is a mentor, guide, partner and advisor, and how it gave him confidence and belief in his career choice, he found this expectation of unquestioning servitude from some of these people confronting. In the US the player was undoubtedly the star, but the caddy's role was valued and celebrated. In Europe for many years now it was seen as a critical role and very much a partnership. In Australia often it was just two mates enjoying the ride together and sharing as teammates the wins and supporting each other through the lean times. This was something else, and it was definitely not for him.

On the bus to the airport, Dave mulled over this experience. He completed the two week assignment, but it was the first time that caddying had felt like work to him. Until this trip, every minute he had spent on the course in practice, preparation, and tournament play had been a privilege for Dave. To be paid well to do this felt like winning the lottery each week. He had still been caddying and was well remunerated in South Korea, but the big difference was in the interactions with the player and her entourage. There wasn't any two way communication, merely directives and the tone was demeaning. The absence of genuine positive feedback really affected him, and he made a mental note of how it made him feel. He thought about how there must be millions of people feeling miserable in the work they do, not because of the type of labour but because of the way they are treated in the workplace. While the concept of "earning a living" is a standard rationalisation and people do endure working to fund the rest of their lifestyle, and economic realities can limit your options, if your job is an enjoyable part of your life then you are very fortunate. The extrinsic rewards you receive from working need to be balanced and in harmony with the intrinsic rewards. Doing what you love never feels like a job it is a joy. His thoughtful review made him feel a little better and affirmed he was indeed a lucky man. He looked forward to getting back out on tour in a fortnight more appreciative and motivated than ever.

Travelling to a place for the first time and observing uniquely different cultures was always interesting and while he appreciated the opportunity, Dave was pleased to be leaving South Korea. The last two weeks had been trying, and when he made his connection in Hong Kong from the Cathay Pacific flight out of Seoul to Qantas Flight 98 to Brisbane, he had never enjoyed the welcoming Australian accents of the cabin crew as much as he did this time. As strongly as he had felt like a detainee when he was holed up in that crowded room during the storm, he now felt like a free man again, safe in the imagined sovereignty of his own private little embassy in the night sky, hurtling back to paradise at 38,000 feet.

Finding the right rhythm and pace for your game sounds simple enough, but a player needs to understand what their optimum tempo is first. We may admire the rhythm and tempo of another player and try to emulate it, but it doesn't mean it is right for us. Many people talk glowingly about the languid movements and timing of Fred Couples or Ernie Els,

7ᵀᴴ HOLE

A strategic intent is essential but must be seen as fluid, continually shifting and evolving. It's directional but not cast in stone forever. It would be a rare person who had lived a life that was an exact reflection of their early dreams and plans, and if such a person existed their life would have been colourless and predictable, and they would have missed the best bits. Predictability is only useful when attributed to an opponent, never yourself. As we navigate through our fourth decade, we are still young enough to remember the journey so far, but mature enough to anticipate the happy detours now ahead of us. There are many ways to play the holes still to come. Surprises and variability are welcome travel companions.

In business, regular reviews against budget are critical. Following an assessment against the previously agreed targets, the business plan and the overall strategies are challenged and if necessary adjusted. Some businesses use the term RIF (revised income forecast) which is a quarterly recasting of the budget. It is prudent and sound practice to make sure that resources and effort aren't wasted on initiatives that will not deliver the original objectives. Everything is always in a state of flux, the market, the competition, the regulatory environment, and the political landscape so why would responsible business leaders lock in their plans, budgets, and investments and rigidly refuse to adjust any of them throughout the business cycle? Most don't, especially with the sophisticated information systems and metrics employed these days, although the timing of the responses are often criticised for being too late and there are a myriad of reasons for this. Any reluctance is predominantly emotional and ego-driven, with the vested interests and reputations of key players influencing decision making.

To stubbornly stick to the original idea and action plan is a trait seen even more prominently in life choices, we rarely review and challenge our decisions correctly. In golf, such obstinacy has wrecked many a round. A player can mistake intransigence as a resolute commitment to their game plan. What if the game plan is wrong? What if the conditions change or the players' capability on the day is not at the usual standard? A perceived attribute can quickly become a liability. There is plenty of merit in the phrase "If it ain't broke don't fix it." Any unnecessary meddling is always going to be problematic, but you do still need to know when it is broken, why it is broken and importantly you have to know how to fix it.

"Has he got eyes in the back of his fucking head?"

Only an Australian member of the gallery would brazenly shout this response to the caddy of a visiting star player. Position, either on the social ladder or the world rankings, never impressed Aussie crowds. Your performance, your character and your humility, and of course the much-loved larrikin nature were the important attributes to earn any reverence or hero worship over here. I was in the gallery the day when a former US Open winner was playing at The Lakes in Sydney at the back end of his peak playing years. The second hole is a par 5 and I was standing behind the green as he hit a nice second shot into the green but it ran across the corner of the green and trickled into the bunker into a poor lie. As he arrived, not having seen it from the fairway, he was visibly frustrated. As he stepped into the bunker, his caddy began frantically gesturing to a couple of blokes back down the fairway who were crossing to the next hole. I estimate they were about 120 metres away and directly behind him as he prepared to play the shot. They ignored the caddy and kept walking so the caddy told his player to wait and he yelled to the spectators to stop moving and to be quiet. That's when the caddy, and the rest of us around the green, got the strident response bellowing up the fairway. The crowd burst into laughter and a few applauded. The caddy was not impressed at all, but to his credit, the US tour veteran had a little chuckle and then hit a beautiful shot to about two feet and made the birdie. As he walked off, he put his sunglasses on the back off his head much to the crowd's delight, and I think we all appreciated his little joke more than his skillful bunker shot. He could easily have been annoyed by the incident, but his handling of the situation and his self-deprecating humour won over the crowd that day.

Rod Hazelbrook had just hit his tee shot on the 8th hole when he turned to his caddy and said,

"I felt something tear in my bicep Davey."

His play through the last couple of tour events had been steady, one top twenty and tied for 34th the previous week. Both he and Dave believed his game was getting sharper and in practice this week he had shot 65 and then 68, 70 and 68 for his first three rounds putting him within striking distance of the leaders. He was 2 under through 7 holes in the final round when the injury occurred.

"Do you think it is serious? Can you go on?" Dave worriedly asked him.

"I'm not sure; let me see how this hole goes." Th
concerned Dave. The US Open was in two weeks, and if Ro
aggravated the injury, he might risk missing the second major
of the year. However, his season so far had been mediocre,
and he badly needed the ranking points and prize money to
secure his standing for the second half of the season, and he
was in an excellent position with 10 holes to go. Rod set up
to hit his second shot into the par 5, a hole he had birdied
every day so far this week. As he hit his 3 wood, Dave sensed
and heard the discomfort, and the ball squirted low and
left well short of the green. It's incredible how the body will
always subconsciously protect an injury no matter how hard
you try to play through the pain. Dave looked at Rod and
noticed the steely look on his face, and he thought he also
looked a little pale. He was obviously processing a lot of the
same thoughts, so Dave decided not to say anything until
they reached the ball. The next shot was a perfect distance
for a gap wedge, but they agreed he should hit a smooth,
knocked down pitching wedge. He flinched a little as he
apprehensively swung at the ball and he didn't catch it that
well but it found the fringe of the green about 30 feet from
the hole. As they walked up the hill, Rod said quietly,

"I didn't feel any pain on that one." Dave nodded at him
and smiled unconvincingly. He knew that between them
they must make the right decision, there was so much at
stake, his mind was racing through his usual process, but it

every movement." The tournament physio reassured them both with his opinion.

"Can I do any further damage if I play on today?" Rod asked directly.

"I don't believe so, but it is probably a good idea to get a scan tomorrow just to be sure. Just use the swing that doesn't hurt!" The physio winked and walked off with a grin. Dave knew he was just trying to lighten the mood, but he almost laughed out loud because it reminded him of the old joke, "Doc it hurts when I do this........" But as with the joke, there was some simple logic in the quip.

"Rod, why don't we leave the driver in the bag this nine and hit those low running long irons you play so well? Let's just get it in play the rest of the day, this course isn't massively long. Does it matter that much if we are hitting 6 or 7 irons into the greens instead of 8 or 9?"

"Ok let's do it."

It was a good test for them both for the rest of the round. They had to adjust the approach to each hole as if it was a new course and Rod was consistently around 40 metres short of his playing partner on each fairway, but Dave was impressed with Rod's application and focus. He never once suggested trying the driver or 3 wood. One birdie and one bogey on the back nine and he finished with a two-under 70, four behind the winner but it gave him a 5th place finish and the much-needed points and a decent cheque. An injury scare and a couple of hours of concern had been turned into a satisfying outcome and a positive learning experience.

"Hitting it that short is good practice for the senior tour Rod." Dave gave Rod a good-natured dig as they walked off the 18th."

"Actually I thought it gave me the chance to see what it's like playing from where you hit it." They walked to the scorer's hut beaming with their arms around each other's shoulders.

8ᵀᴴ HOLE

There are significantly more good days in your life than bad ones, even if the ratio has been skewed to the negative by your attitude. Likewise in a round of golf, you will play more good shots than poor ones, no matter how badly you believe you are playing. By good shots I mean where you leave yourself in a good position, still with options or you have made the right decision and executed correctly, not only those rare great shots. By the time you reach the eighth hole enough golf has been played to measure and appreciate the positive elements of your round, but there's still enough golf left to play to ruin your day if you predominantly focus on the things that have gone wrong.

"That's what you get! There's a price and a dividend for every action." Dave thought that was a strange way to put it, but it made good sense to him. He had been listening to a couple of veterans on tour chatting near the putting green at Valhalla. He was in Kentucky for the Senior PGA event, and he was caddying for a player he had met at a pro-am celebrity event a year or so ago. This guy had been a good amateur when he was young but despite having dreams of playing on the pro tour; he instead pursued a business career. He had done well enough to retire quite early and was able to commit himself to golf again, and after three years of trying, he finally earned his card for the senior tour. He was having much more fun now than he ever did in the corporate world. He'd managed to qualify for this major event, but unfortunately, his caddy had decided to retire for health reasons recently. Rod was taking a few weeks off for the birth of his first child, so the timing worked out for both of them, and Dave happily agreed to be on his bag this week. He was looking forward to it as he enjoyed Graham's company and his storytelling and there was the added benefit of getting to see some of the legends of the game inside the ropes. It should be a fun week. The tournament was being sponsored by Brown Forman, the makers of Jack Daniels and they were well known as a company that epitomised southern hospitality and took enormous pride in the way they entertained their guests. It was one of those events where Dave almost felt guilty getting paid to be involved, well maybe not guilty but mildly embarrassed and very grateful.

"I hear what you're saying Ken, I've seen quite a bit of it the last few years. Just last month in New Orleans I heard an executive from one of the sponsor companies complaining that he invited two important clients to play in the pro-am with him, and the young pro in the group barely spoke to them all day. He just focused on his practice with his caddy, and left for the range as soon as the round was over."

The conversation Dave had overheard continued, Ken had been relaying the story about how one of the young players had missed a golden opportunity by not engaging with a guest at his table at the tournament dinner, who it turns out was looking to support a player financially. He owned a huge PR firm and could have helped the player.

"Paul, do you remember when we first came out on tour? It was drummed into us by the older guys and the tour officials that the sponsors and the paying public were the most important people to the tour. It was expected of us to do everything we could to welcome them and make their experience memorable and enjoyable. The thing was that most of the pro-am players were successful and prominent business people, and some of the connections I made have been very beneficial, plus I have made some terrific friends over the years. Without the people attending or watching on TV there were no sponsors and without them no prizemoney. I may sound like an old fart now, but perhaps there is just too much money around today." Ken said sadly, shaking his head.

"Maybe Ken, but most of the young kids though are excellent, I've been impressed with many of them, the game still has a positive effect on players, it's just a small number who have lost sight of what is so important and so wonderful about this game."

"Thank goodness for that Paul, you're right, there's still a lot more decent stuff happening around us than bad, just like the world we live in, but the negative elements get all the headlines and focus."

"Play well today."

"You too buddy." They shook hands and went back to their preparations.

Dave observed with interest the contrast in attitudes between Graham and the seasoned pros that had spent decades playing under pressure on tour. He was just grateful and over the moon to be out here and didn't sweat the mistakes and small things as much as many of the pros. Some seemed a little jaded and gave the impression that it was drudgery, a job they had to do, and every misfortune or mistake became a major annoyance. Curiously the well-known stars were more relaxed, perhaps because of the level of consistent success they had enjoyed, for them, it looked almost as if they were at a fun reunion. The journeymen players though had spent their whole careers struggling to make cuts and earn enough money to retain their cards, and it was clear that many were now on the senior tour trying to make amends for opportunities they believed they had missed on the regular tour and were still grinding hard. Whereas Graham was like a little kid on Christmas morning enjoying all of it, full of wonder and joy.

Without the big names though there would be no senior tour as the public wanted to see their heroes from the past playing. Primarily for nostalgic reasons, like watching an ageing rock star performing one last time where both the artist and the audience can recall the glory days of their youth, but Dave sensed another reason as well. Listening to the conversations amongst the spectators at a senior event was distinctly different to the regular tour. When watching the younger players the sounds and comments from the gallery indicated just how well they understood the gulf between their own games and that of the powerful young guns. They watch on amazed at the distances and height these players achieve, full well knowing that they could never hit the ball like that. But as the strength and physical abilities of the senior players begin to lessen with age, the amateurs outside the ropes start to entertain the idea that the skill level of the seniors may just be coming within reach of their own ability. Dave was hearing comments all day suggesting as much,

"He hit seven iron there when I played here last year I hit an eight." A proud punter would say to his mate.

"Yes, you may well have," Dave thought to himself, "but it was probably the best eight iron of your life, and you came out of your shoes to reach the green down breeze, the pro was hitting a smooth cut seven iron into a hurting cross breeze."

There would be no such comparative comments if the six foot four, 22-year-old world number three hit a pitching wedge into the same green. It shouldn't matter anyway, the number you write on your card is always more important than the number stamped on the bottom of the club. Pros know this, and any comparisons are pointless as equipment is continually changing including the lofts, today's nine irons have lofts similar to eight or even seven irons from the past. The reality, however, is that the skill gap is still far too wide for all but the very best of the elite amateurs to match it with the senior tour players, but the dreams are encouraged because it sells tickets. If the horizon can be seen and almost touched by the dreamer, then they will most certainly want a closer look. That is one of the attractions of the senior tour; golfers can imagine themselves out there, that and a fond glance backward at the past.

Graham started the tournament well and was two under through the front nine, but he hit a couple of loose shots starting the back nine and bogeyed 10 and 11. Occasionally, though not as common as in other sports, there will be a loudmouth, normally emboldened by one too many beverages, who unfortunately believes he has the right to heckle a player. This day, for whatever reason, one such guy chose Graham as his target in the first round. After the sloppy bogey on 10 and all the way up 11, this clown decided to let everyone know about Graham's lack of experience and started rhetorically asking questions out loud,

"Why should nobodies be allowed to play in a major? Who wants to watch these guys, I could have seen this in the pro-am."

After a series of similar questions and statements, by the time they had reached the 12th tee, Dave had heard enough and parts of the crowd were now becoming frustrated and angry and had started to respond to the guy. It was getting a little tense. Suddenly Dave dropped the bag and walked directly over to him. When he reached him, he put his hand on his shoulder. The crowd was hushed as they anticipated a physical confrontation. What happened next surprised everybody. He said to the heckler,

"Obviously you love golf, or you wouldn't have paid to be here, but something has upset you. How about I extend a courtesy to you and then you reciprocate and give my player the respect he deserves for qualifying for this major? Do we have an agreement?"

The question was posed with a force and tone of voice that sounded more like a command. Instead of having him thrown out of the tournament, disrupting play and producing differing opinions amongst the gallery (there's always someone who disagrees with that action) Dave let him carry the bag for a hole, which diffused the situation although there were a couple of people in the gallery who gave the heckler a piece of their mind. The media coverage went viral! After the players complete the 12th hole, the guy is smiling broadly, he goes up to Graham and offers his apologies, shakes his hand, and walks away to cheers and laughter from the crowd a changed man. I am sure he carried with him memories and a story to tell his friends and family for years to come. The biggest ovation from the gallery was for Dave as they walked onto the 13th tee, he earned their appreciation by doing the exact opposite of the usual procedure in these circumstances. He leaned towards Graham and said with a wink,

"Guess you aren't a nobody anymore!"

Dave and Graham worked their way around the rest of the challenging but picturesque Valhalla golf course. Once or twice Graham attempted to take on a risky shot, reasoning to Dave that he might not get to play a Senior PGA again and he wanted to make the most of it.

"I understand that," Dave calmly said, "but let's try and make the cut first and play all four rounds this week." A good example was on the island green 13th. Graham wanted to hit his tee shot right to the end of the fairway and leave himself a short flick with a lob wedge. But Dave knew that the six bunkers on the left of the fairway in the driving zone must be avoided at all costs because a shot from one of them or in between them in the thick rough was extremely difficult. He convinced Graham to lay back short of the danger and hit a fuller shot into the green. Graham made birdie and gave Dave a nod of thanks as they trudged up the hill to the elevated 14th tee. He played the last five holes in even par to post a respectable 71, and despite missing a makeable birdie putt on the par 5 18th, both caddy and player were very satisfied with the day's work. Dave saw the camera crews before Graham did and gave him a heads up as they walked off the back of the green. Though they did interview Graham who was enjoying the attention, the media was more interested in talking to Dave. He waved them off as he headed to the clubhouse.

"Still got some work to do guys, excuse me if I get to it." He said modestly.

"Why did you decide to ask that heckler inside the ropes?" One reporter shouted at him, although that was pretty much what they were all asking him. He paused for a moment and turned to the media scrum without putting the bag down. He said plainly,

"A big mouth yobbo is stronger on the sidelines, put them in the spotlight, and they're out of their comfort zone, take them on head to head, and they feed off the confrontation but move the focus onto them in a different way, they may even learn something. In Australia, we say that if you are going to throw shit at somebody remember you still have to stick your hands in the manure first."

The crowd around the interview erupted, but as he walked away despite all the noise Dave heard someone say to one of the reporters,

"What's a yobbo?"

Graham came up beside Dave and asked,

"What the hell does that Australian saying mean?"

"I have no bloody idea; I just made it up!" They both laughed so hard they had tears in their eyes.

If we think back throughout our lives, there will most likely be numerous situations that may have turned out better if we had tried a different approach to reach a solution, to produce an outcome that was mutually beneficial and didn't permanently damage a relationship or burn a bridge. Forgiveness is difficult especially when you have been hurt, mistreated or wronged, but it is hard because it is so important. It also does not excuse the actions and behaviour of the other person, just as the rowdy spectator wasn't excused for his boorish behaviour. Hopefully, he learned a lesson from the experience. If Dave had aggressively attacked him instead, he would have no doubt used that as justification for his actions and maybe repeated it with another player in the future. Forgiveness provides the person doing the forgiving permission to move forward and release the pain and bitterness; it doesn't let the wrongdoer off the hook. And it is not weak by any means, it takes a lot of strength to do it and sincerely mean it, I am sure Dave wanted to pull that bloke's nose at Valhalla, but he rose above it and made a positive impact on a large number of people.

9TH HOLE

Frustration can lead to a conclusion that you need to change something to get the results you desire. A golfer will immediately start considering new equipment or lessons to alter their swing if they have been playing poorly. A strange amnesia occurs as all the good play of the past is forgotten. The same clubs that delivered a win in the monthly medal or that cherished hole in one are determined to now be the prime cause of the current loss of form and thus mentally abandoned forever to be replaced as soon as the budget allows. As you complete the first nine, a quick mental review of play so far frequently evokes the idea that an immediate change is required. A different ball, a new strategy, or change of swing thought is often employed. The mid-round re-evaluation is reminiscent of the midlife crisis.

The fall-back plan for the struggling golfer is the steadfast conviction that once we have the latest gear, more practice is all that is required to scale the heights of golfing achievements. We have all heard players say,

"If only I had a few more hours to practice each week I would be in A grade."

Then there are the low markers who regularly play well at their home club, who possess the unshakable belief that if they were able to have access to the latest equipment as soon as it is developed and time for unlimited practice then they would be on tour. The extended logic to all of this is that they know that the tour players do indeed practice for hours and hours every day, so if they could also put in long hours on the practice range and get their hands on the newest products then naturally their game would approach similar levels of expertise. Yet we can all buy the products now that were the latest and greatest on tour last season. Have you ever hit a great drive or holed an exceptional putt only to have your playing partner immediately grab your driver or putter and examine it with the intensity of a forensic scientist looking for the clues to its power? It is an unusual phenomenon that seems to be more prominent in golf than any other sport, despite it being one of the hardest games to master. People don't automatically believe that if they practiced more they could win a gold medal in the 100 metres at the Olympics, or meet Roger Federer in the final at Wimbledon. Not many

40-year-olds entertain the idea that if they could train every day, they could run out for QLD in the State of Origin. I've never heard a friend say that if they could find the time to work on their technique a perfect 10 on the parallel bars is guaranteed. Similarly, in professions that require creativity, knowledge, and talent, no one assumes that it is only time invested or new equipment that assures a place at the top of their field. No matter how much intense rehearsing a person does, they can never open their mouth and create a sound that moves people like Pavarotti, Don Henley or Adele unless they are blessed with an incredible singing voice. People naturally accept that some people are born with a particular ability.

However, in golf, there seems to be a frequent disregard for the amount of natural ability that is needed in the first place to allow skills to be honed to world-class standard as if it is possible to become a tour player making millions of dollars merely with a prescribed amount of effort. If it was that simple everybody would be doing it. Yes you need to work hard to play golf at the highest level, and all players can improve with more of the right practice, but banging away on the range, repeating the same old technique will not automatically transform you into a scratch golfer. Nor will the latest driver designed with NASA technology and materials.

It is possible to waste a talent by not practising enough but you can't create a talent by over practising!

These ambitious dreams to become a better player, however, keep the equipment manufacturers and instructors in business. The passionate desire to continually improve is nevertheless, a positive element of the game, and part of the attraction, although in some cases you might say an obsession, and so the pursuit is a commendable endeavour, but you need to attempt to reach your own highest level of performance and chase realistic targets.

An enjoyable aspect of golf is that because it is a game you can play for life and it is regulated by a handicap system, then theoretically any player could compete with the top players in the world in a social or club event. The pro would have to use a handicap of around plus 5 or 6.

The compulsion to make changes if we aren't satisfied or happy exists in our lives as well. At different times, no doubt we have all thought about changing our job, dropping a habit, redesigning our routines, starting new plans, shifting where we live and in extreme cases seeking a new partner. I wonder how many people stop and analyse why they feel unfulfilled before making any significant adjustments to their lifestyle or living conditions, rather than risk suffering the regrets that may come later from impetuous choices. Spontaneity is excellent, but foresight is a wonderfully effective preventive for the pain of hindsight.

Rod Hazelbrook had played well most of the season and was securely within the top 50 in the world rankings which gave him entry to all the majors and world championship events. Yet his record in these events had been disappointing. His best finish was tied 28th in the British Open. He had missed more cuts than he had made in the premier events and felt he needed to make some changes to go to the next level. This concerned Dave greatly. Change is warranted if you know exactly where and why you have a deficiency and it is possible to achieve the improvement you seek. You see Dave believed the problem was predominantly mental, but Rod felt it was mechanical and equipment related. When he heard he was trialling different putters and drivers, plus he was testing new shafts in his irons and talking to a new swing coach, Dave knew it was time for a discussion.

"Seriously Rod even if you gain some improvement if you have changed multiple things how do you know which one has been effective? Is it the swing changes, the new clubs or the different shafts? And if it breaks down under pressure what do you do then? Let's at least do one at a time."

For the first time since being hired as Rod's full-time caddy, Dave was expressing his frustration. Dave knew that Rod was a natural player, and if he got overly technical he might lose his feel, but he also understood his concerns. He was 37 now and had never really contended in a major. The same guys he could compete with and regularly defeat on the regular events always seemed to have his measure in the majors. He desperately wanted to win a tournament that would define his career, so much so that he tightened up and tried too hard and because the courses were difficult and set up to challenge players, he tended to play conservatively and at times tried to "steer" his shots into the right positions. He needed to just let it go on the course and accept a few bogeys because he would make more birdies that way.

"Davey, I have to find a way to contend in these events, and I need to do it quickly."

He was as tense as Dave had ever seen before.

"Why the sudden urgency mate?"

"The little fella is nearly three, and I want to be based back in Australia by the time he starts school. He can travel with us now but once school starts both he and Donna will need to be based at home, and I'll be away for most of the year, and I don't think I could cope with that. I would miss too many of those precious times, plus we would like to have another child, and we both want our children to be born in Australia." Despite the softness of Rod's voice the raw emotion was powerful.

Dave was very quiet for a few minutes. The simple honesty from Rod caught him off guard. That he trusted Dave enough to talk from the heart and they had a relationship that allowed such intimacy touched him deeply, and his silence was caused in equal parts by contemplation and admiration.

"Davey I want so badly to win a big tournament or at least be in with a chance coming down the stretch Sunday afternoon, but I can't keep chasing it at the expense of seeing my son grow up. My Dad worked long hours and travelled a lot when I was young, and I hardly saw him, we never really got to know each other until I was an adult and he had retired. So I've made a promise to Donna and importantly to myself, I've got a deadline, two more years and then I'm done playing full time in America."

Finally, Dave spoke.

"Ok Rod, that's 8 majors, 2 Players championships and 8 World Golf Championships. Let's get to work I have some ideas. We can discuss them over dinner; I'm cooking, do you like beef cheeks? You bring the wine, and of course the family!"

It was an enjoyable dinner, and Dave was pleased that Rod seemed to relax a little as they discussed their early ideas about how to achieve his objective. Donna was also relieved to hear there was an end to their time apart on the horizon. After Rod and his family had left Dave was sitting by himself lost in his thoughts and enjoying one last glass of wine. He was pleased they had been able to discuss Rod's worries openly and were now working on a plan. His mind started to drift gently to a quiet place, and he was almost dozing off when he heard someone clearly say to him,

"What do you expect of yourself?"

Being half asleep, it startled him. While it still amazed him when this happened, this time he was also a little frustrated. Though he had no idea where that voice he kept hearing came from, nor did he know who it was, Dave had been energised by the mystery. Early on he had tried to analyse who it might be. Was is it his conscience, or was he having a mental breakdown? Could it be from another dimension or maybe even God? Then one night in a moment of clarity he realised that it didn't matter who or what it was. All that mattered was the meaning and how it affected him, what he did after hearing the messages was far more important than who had said it. Seve was right. He was still exasperated, however, because he only ever got questions, never answers. Isn't that the point? If you are lucky enough to receive such communication shouldn't you get important answers? "Don't ask, just tell me," he thought to himself, it would save a lot of time. He was annoyed at himself as well. He knew he was a little hard on Rod and should have understood his state of mind much earlier, and Dave felt he should grasp the meaning of these messages better than he was. He stumbled off to bed confused and unsettled.

The next morning Dave was driving into town for an appointment with his accountant, he needed to make some adjustments to his superannuation plan. Coincidently there was an advertisement playing on the radio about financial planning for your retirement, the tag line was, "where do you see yourself in forty years?" Suddenly the realisation hit him so forcefully that he had to pull over. Of course he was being given questions rather than answers. A question is a beginning, it prompts you to think, and it's limitless. An answer instructs you, has a limit and is an ending.

An answer only has a single outcome, but a question can motivate you to explore many paths and alternatives.

Dave immediately started to consider last night's question. What was his expectation of himself? He began to seriously evaluate his own goals and dreams, and most importantly how he believed he should be living and conducting himself both personally and professionally.

10TH HOLE

*Loyalty and trust, to not only the important
people in your life but also to the tried and tested
ways of doing things are becoming less fashionable
and less apparent in a world that desires quick
results and immediate gratification. As we get
older, at a time when we should reasonably be
allowed to settle into routines of comfortable and
skilled activity, we are thrust into an unsettling
atmosphere in which we feel compelled to prove
ourselves continually. If something or someone
used to work well why do we see the sudden
urgency to abandon it at the first sign of a drop
in performance these days?*

Friends can often take on the role of a pseudo caddy
by providing encouragement, praise, and feedback,
acting as a sounding board and giving others a sense
of belonging that is such a powerful psychological need. The
good natured ribbing and practical jokes also play a part. As

essential and nurturing as friends are, they aren't, however, as invested in the results as much as a caddy or a spouse unless they have a common objective or benefit materially from a joint project. Nor are they always seen by the individual as qualified or as credible as a caddy, who is usually employed for their knowledge and capability. The principle has a few variations and combinations. For example, a spouse may be unsupportive or even critical, but they're still impacted negatively or positively by the outcome of their partners' endeavours. An altruistic stranger may offer useful advice and guidance from their own experiences but has no interest in benefitting personally from their efforts. Members of a team have common goals and shared results, but the support isn't as focussed one on one as that from a caddy, and there exists an expected reciprocity to the teammates. Players rarely help or directly encourage the caddies to do their job well. Remuneration, appreciation and ongoing employment are the rewards for the expected level of performance. The role of a caddy figure is unique. It can have elements of the relationship between friends or loved ones but has a foundation built on the employer, employee contract. A contract, however, that can be broken with less difficulty and without the complications associated with ending a friendship or relationship.

In recent times there has emerged a disturbing trend that is a threat to anyone in a leadership position and charged with the responsibility for performance and results. CEO's political leaders, sporting coaches and yes, even caddies are suffering the same fates. How often now do we see coaches being sacked because the team has lost a few games? This normally involves paying out their contracts at considerable cost to the club, mid-season disruption, players splintering into groups, Board disagreements or even spills, and unhappy fans. Not to mention the challenging task of convincing a successor to take on the challenge of walking into a club in turmoil. Rarely though do you see players being replaced or punished to the same extent as the coach, even though they are the ones on the field. Paradoxically most of the coaches who are terminated nearly always get picked up by another club eventually, which begs the question if they performed poorly enough to be dumped mid-contract why would another club hire them? Apparently, the desire for change overrides past performance and ability. It is almost farcical with coaches being forced to play a game of musical chairs with their careers as they move from club to club replacing other coaches who have been moved on just as they were themselves.

This "scapegoat" mentality is spreading into every part of society. Political leaders who were previously seen as the new saviour enjoying enthusiastic support from their party, the media and their electorate at the beginning, are quickly dumped when polls shift. CEOs get replaced if profits or share prices fall slightly. The accepted view nowadays is that rapidly introducing something or someone new will fix the current problems. It's very unfair to the incumbents; they deserve some time to prove themselves and grow into their position. Nobody is afforded any time for trial and error anymore which has always been a valuable learning tool. Experience is not built on successes alone, often the most powerful lessons come from failure, but in our current world, it's get results or get out.

It's reminiscent of the golfer struggling with poor form who looks to new equipment, a new swing, and even a new caddy to improve their play. A number of high profile players have replaced long-serving caddies lately. In some cases, the partnerships had achieved multiple major wins and reached high positions in the world rankings, as high as number one for a few of them, so it's hardly a lack of performance or know how. Obviously, relationships can run their course, and a fresh change may be necessary, but generally in each of these situations, the decision has been predicated on a sustained period of poor form. So the player is looking for improvement and feels a new caddy will produce better play, despite the successful track record. So what has changed and what will change? There's an epidemic of people applying short-term overreactions to hopefully address a longer-term problem. Continuity is reassuring psychologically, yet there is less and less of that comfort around for us to rely on.

Australian players and caddies tend to stick together on the overseas tours, offering the support of a travelling social group that provides a small lifeline to the Aussie lifestyle and helps them cope with the challenges of being a long way from home and loved ones for much of the year. The lifestyle looks glamourous, but anyone who has travelled a lot for their work will tell you that the gloss comes off very quickly when you are living in hotels and crammed into crowded airports and planes much of the time, spending a surprisingly considerable amount of time eating and travelling alone. I must have spent thousands of nights in hotels travelling for business, and you are presented with two unpalatable choices. Eating alone in your room or sitting in a restaurant, miserable because you are on your own but dreading some pushy stranger wanting to join you at the table. At night I got into a bad routine of sleeping with the television on just to hear some voices, a habit that sadly still exists today. Often the worst loneliness is felt when you are surrounded by strangers. The ache for a friendly word or touch from someone you care about and who cares about you unconditionally seems stronger when you are swept up in a surging crowd of faceless people, unsettling you with their unwelcome jostling and noise. I rarely had other Australians with me, so at least I suppose the people on the golf tour have that benefit, and many of them are travelling to the same cities and tour stops each week together. That's why then if someone is cast out for any reason, the pain is compounded. It is like being stranded in a foreign place robbed of your identity and purpose, without the means or method to get home. It can happen to a player if they lose their card or status and it happens to a caddy if they are abruptly fired.

"Dave did you hear what happened to Matty?" Pete said rather seriously. Dave looked up from the golf bag he was emptying and shook his head.

"Ron Alderley sacked him straight after he missed the cut at the Byron Nelson."

"Did you hear why?" Dave asked.

"Not sure but he gave him the old, it's not you it's me speech, saying he didn't want the relationship to be damaged by continuing to work together, what a weak cop-out," Pete said this with a look on his face as if he had just tasted something foul.

"I know both Ron and Matt well; I can't believe Ron would do that." Dave said genuinely shocked.

"Maybe you can speak to Ron?" Pete suggested hopefully.

"Possibly, I'll see." Dave walked off thinking this is terrible timing for Matty; his wife is seven months pregnant. There's never a good time to lose your job, and though the top caddies may earn a very good living, he was worried about his mate. Ron hadn't been playing well for the last three years barely keeping his card, and yet Matt had stuck with him even though his own income would have been affected by the drop in form. A lot of people think that caddies have a great job, being inside the ropes at significant events, travelling all around the world and they only have to carry the player's bag. There is a lot more to the job than most people know. A caddy must also make all of their own travel arrangements each week and wear the cost while travelling economy at the blunt end of the plane and staying in cheap hotels or shared accommodation. They don't get the access or privileges that players do at the events, and still have all the stress of performing under pressure to make cuts that the players do, although at only 10% of the players' income. Plus they are depending on someone else to play well enough to provide their livelihood. Worst of all they can be fired at any time with no protection or recourse. Dave wasn't sure that he was that recourse.

"Hey Matt, how are you doing?" Matt lived in the same city as Dave, so when he got home from the tournament, Dave had called Matt and asked him to meet him for a beer.

"Not too bad Davey, still a little stunned, but maybe it's a blessing. At least now I can stay with Maree for the last part of the pregnancy, I was worried about not being around." Matt was trying to put a positive spin on the situation, but Dave could sense the hurt he was feeling.

"Could you see it coming at all?" Dave tried to tease out a little more information.

"Well as everyone knows he hasn't played well for

quite a while, and it was getting to him. He had started experimenting with changes of equipment, and his attitude was becoming worse every week. I believed he just needed to adjust his state of mind. When I raised it with him it got very heated, and we had a blazing row. I told him he needed to lose the attitude and he decided he needed to lose the caddy."

As bad as this was Dave reasoned that it had been mainly an angry overreaction after a long build-up. Maybe it was recoverable if they both cooled down. Dave wanted to speak with Ron but felt he should run it by Matt first.

"Are you ok if I have a chat to Ron?

"Yeah that's fine, I'm not sure it will help though he was pretty worked up. You know, the part that bothers me the most is that it's not just the job, I thought we were mates. Now with this decision, he affects not only my finances and reputation but my wife and child's future as well. Plus he has taken something away from me that I love doing, and the thing is I don't reckon I've done anything wrong!"

The frustration Matt was feeling was evident, his voice was wavering and his eyes revealed the pain; Dave thought he was on the verge of tears.

"Let me try Matt, you take it easy mate, I'll call you after I speak with him. Give my best to Maree." Dave said with a smile that he tried his best to make look reassuring. He wasn't sure he pulled it off.

"Ok, thanks Davey," Matt walked away looking lost and broken.

Dave wasn't able to catch up with Ron for a couple of weeks until they were both at the same event. He could have called him, but he felt it was important to have this discussion in person. He left a message for Ron suggesting they catch up for a beer after the Wednesday pro-am. To Ron's credit, he turned up even though Dave was sure he knew what they would be discussing. Dave had known Ron for years and had spent quite a bit of time with him on the Australian circuit. Dave liked him, he called a spade a spade but in recent times he had been getting a reputation for being disagreeable company on the course and unpleasant socially, especially if he had a few drinks. Dave knew that changes in personality or attitude generally have a deeper cause, and he wasn't sure it was for him to be digging into Ron's personal matters, but if it came out he would be delicate, but he wasn't going to take any of his rubbish either.

"Hi Ron, how's things mate." Dave greeted him warmly, and they shook hands.

"I'm ok Dave what's happening?" By this Ron meant I know why you've called me here so let's get to it.

"Ok Ron I'm sure you know I wanted to talk about Matty, and I appreciate you agreeing to meet. What happened between you two?"

"Dave you know these things happen from time to time,

every player-caddy relationship runs its course. It's time for a fresh start." Ron said in a tired tone.

"I know but couldn't you have phased it over some time to let Matt get another job lined up, it was so sudden he just feels blindsided. Plus he feels let down he thought you were mates."

"We are that's why I did it like this." A hint of frustration could be heard in Ron's voice. Dave thought he heard something else. But as he was trying to process this answer and what he had meant, Ron raised his beer to his lips, and Dave saw some webbing and gauze under Ron's right arm. He pointed at it and said.

"What have you done to yourself Ron?" Thinking he must have injured himself. Ron looked straight at him with a mixture of resignation and trepidation on his face and said softly,

"Davey, I've got cancer. I have to wear a pump for the medication. What you can see is a bandage holding it in place firmly enough for me to swing the club." Dave was stunned he couldn't even answer. Ron continued,

"I had to end it like that with Matty, he needs to get on another player's bag. It's not looking good for me; I won't be able to stay out here much longer. You know him Dave, if I told him he would have never left me, he would have wanted to help me to the end. I just couldn't see him miss the chance of getting another job at this time of year. Anyway, I think

I've found him someone, the guy is going to call him this week."

"Bloody hell Ron, is there anything I can do mate?" Dave was struggling to even get the words out.

"Just one thing, don't tell Matty about this, or anyone else for that matter. I want to stay out here long enough to see him settled with his new player. Then I will make an announcement. Promise me Dave." Ron said this very firmly, but there was a painful pleading in his eyes. He had thought all of this through, Dave had completely misjudged him.

Ron did manage to keep playing long enough for Matt to settle into the new job. Unfortunately he never got the chance to make an announcement. He became very ill after one of the tournaments and lapsed into a coma. He never recovered. At the funeral, Dave took Matt aside and told him the whole story. He broke down in Dave's arms. That night with many other Aussie friends from the tour, they shared beers, stories, tears and a lot of laughter.

11TH HOLE

As little kids, we all rely on the assistance of those close to us for practically everything. If we are fortunate to have caring family around us, we are given shelter, nourishment, and comfort unconditionally. There's always somebody nearby to protect and guide us. As we get a little older other people such as teachers, mentors, sporting coaches, and community leaders fulfil additional supporting roles in our lives as well. However, somewhere along the way, we begin to accept that we must now look after ourselves, and then later learn to provide similar care to our own families. This is the natural order of things, but just because you have a duty of care to others and have learned from experience how to do it, it doesn't mean that you no longer need assistance yourself. That's a common misconception. Just knowing you can talk to someone about your problems and challenges is reassuring. Friends and partners can provide the support if you seek and allow it. In golf, only the elite golfers use a caddy and yet ironically struggling amateurs probably need one more than a professional. Unless you are in a team event, it's against the rules to seek advice from playing partners about club choices and shot strategies, but there's nothing prohibiting discussion about how you are feeling.

Skills and capabilities will diminish with age. It is unavoidable. Players must then leverage their knowledge and experience as their physical gifts wane. Luckily experience cannot be accelerated, and this allows the older player to retain an advantage over younger players in at least one crucial part of the game. The British Open is a good example. Mark O'Meara won the Open at 41, Zach Johnson at 39 and Padraig Harrington at 36. In 2009 Tom Watson, the five-time winner, famously almost won it at the age of 59, only a wicked bounce on the 18th green cost him the chance of a simple two-putt to take the claret jug that year. The prior year Greg Norman at 53, having hardly played any golf that season, was in contention all week and was leading with nine holes to go, only to lose to Harrington who defended his 2007 title. Peter Thomson, like Watson, won 5 times, including

3 years in a row and 4 wins in 5 years. Walter Hagen and Bobby Locke lifted the trophy 4 times each. Faldo, Nicklaus, Woods, Ballesteros, Player, Henry Cotton, and Bobby Jones all won on three occasions. The nuances and difficulty of links golf accentuate the benefits of knowing how to navigate these challenges and how it feels as you do it, hindsight and foresight crashing together to forge a valuable weapon that is only available to the battle-scarred player. Prudence displaces ego over time and the simple sounding phrase "get it in play" takes on so much more meaning when being out of play in this particular tournament can be devastating to a players' chances of winning."

I always felt that I had an unfair advantage when I played in a team event with Davey. This happened quite often because luckily for me whenever he had a couple of weeks off from the tour it invariably coincided with one of the team honour board events at Pelican Waters. To have one of the best caddies on tour who also happens to be an excellent player as your partner, was a tremendous fillip for my chances of winning. We had progressed to the final of the four-ball match play final, and on the practice range a few minutes before our tee time Dave came over to me and said,

"Dougal (this is what Dave calls me sometimes), I have a strategy I want you to follow today. They have more handicap than us, and as the lowest marker, I need you to put some pressure on them. Except for the three or four obvious holes where you have to hit driver, I want you to play first and hit your hybrid and put it in the fairway, no matter how the match is going or what has happened on the previous hole."

"Fair enough Davey but that will leave me some longer shots in on some holes, in this wind today I could be hitting 6 or even 5 irons to some greens."

I'm not sure why I even raised a concern because I had long ago learned to trust his instincts and act on his advice, it may have been because I was a little keyed up for the final.

"It doesn't matter, if you are in the fairway every hole, they will still be expecting you to hit the green and if I go with the driver and get into some attacking positions, the pressure will build on them continually, and they will start to push harder and make a few mistakes. You know Gordo he goes flat out with the driver on every hole, I want him to start thinking about steering a few. Seriously, I have to explain myself to you?" He grinned at me and flicked my cap off my head.

"You do that to Rod at the Masters do you?" I laughed as I bent down to retrieve my cap.

"Only when there are no cameras on us, come on let's go win this thing."

My doubts were unfounded as expected. The match went exactly as Dave had predicted, in fact, it was so close to his plan it was just as if he had written the script and a game plan and handed a copy to all of us on the first tee. They made a fast start utilising their handicap advantage, but Dave made sure we stuck to his strategy. Slowly the pressure started to build on our opponents as we continually put the ball in play. By the back nine, we had the momentum with us, and we reeled in their 3 up lead. Just as forecast, Gordo started to press off the tee and hit a couple into the hazard, which then put extra pressure on his partner to match it with us. We got back to square and were playing the tough par 4 18th hole. I hit my second shot just short of the green, only one of our opponents was still in the hole, he was in the greenside bunker with a tough up and down to make par. Dave had a very long putt for par, and then he did the strangest thing considering the circumstances. He walked up to me and gave me the line on my putt; it was a tricky shot through the fringe and up a slope with a left to right break at the end. If you got it going too far to the right, it would run straight down a slope to twenty feet.

"Your line is that little brown patch 3 feet left of the pin, but you will need to hit it harder than you think up that slope to keep it left of the hole, it flattens out around the hole, and you'll have a straight two-foot putt to win."

With that he then incredibly walked off to the cart, picking up his ball on the way and casually put his putter back in his bag? He didn't even turn around to watch me hit the shot. Even telling me that I would have that putt for a win was odd because by this time Kenny had played a nice shot out of the bunker and had a makeable fifteen footer for par. Well as has happened so often before, I responded to his direction confidently, and the ball rolled up to just over two feet. Kenny's putt grazed the edge of the hole, and as I stood over the ball for that final stroke I glanced at Dave who by now had come up on the green, he had a satisfied look on his face and said to me quietly,

"Let me hear the sound, Dougal."

Later in the clubhouse, as we were celebrating the win I had to ask him.

"Why did you pick up your ball on the last green when you still had a putt for par?"

"Well two reasons actually, firstly I wanted to remove your safety net, I needed you to be thinking that you had no alternative but to hit a quality shot, with no bailouts, but I also was trying to distract you a little and have you wondering why I picked up. The first objective was to focus your intent, and the second to reduce the stress of the moment.

I am continually astonished by Davey's ability to see a clear strategy and then put the plan into action through other people. He has a tremendous gift for motivating people and focussing their efforts on the right actions. He gets you into the moment in the optimum state of mind then makes you feel good about your execution and performance, and he does it in a quiet, understated manner. Tremendous attributes for a caddy but priceless qualities in a close friend.

Everyone has heard the adages that you need to empty the mind and think less to play better. I wonder if it works in reverse, i.e., if you play less you will think better! While I believe that you cannot play well by not thinking at all, there is merit in changing how you think. If you have the mindset that the result doesn't matter, or more accurately if you focus and stress less about the results you most certainly can improve. It's a strange contradiction; you are trying to improve your performance, which is measured by the score, by not caring about the result. But it does work, especially on the greens; you should putt as if you're not worried about missing, and you will find that your first putts are a lot better because you are less tentative. However, it's not so easy to genuinely think like that. It helps if you can find an activity or a situation that allows you to practice getting into that mindset.

"I'm worried about his interview Dave; it's been a little while since I have had one. The last couple of jobs I was approached by somebody from the industry who knew me. That's always a lot easier. Plus I've had a year or so off." I was sitting in Dave's lounge room drinking coffee. I had borrowed his utility to move some furniture, and I had just dropped it back to him.

"Is the job that important?" His reply surprised me; it sounded a little flippant.

"Of course it is what do you mean?" I was sure he had a reason for asking me that.

"I mean do you need this job, financially or for some other reason."

"Well financially no, but I feel like I still have something to offer and as much as I have enjoyed travelling and playing a lot of golf, I've been a little bored, and I miss the industry." I answered him.

"And the responsibility and position," he continued his probing, I felt like the interview had already started. Dave was well aware that I had held a number of CEO roles; some had been problematic, and all were pressurised. In fact, the reason I decided to semi-retire was because of the stress and time away from home. I had also become a little jaded about the lack of values and integrity I had encountered with some of the people I had to deal with. I guess he was concerned that I had left because of burn out, and now he was surprised I would want to go back to all that.

"Yes, I suppose I miss that as well," I said honestly. "I believe, though, that I have the experience that could be very useful to right organisation, particularly one that is growing or facing challenges and I'd love to help them through that transition."

"So your motivations are quite different from when you were younger?" Dave asked seriously.

"That's getting a little deep Davey; you're full of questions aren't you."

"Am I?" he said with a smile.

"Very funny," I said laughing, but he had made an excellent point. This was so dissimilar to when I was climbing the corporate ladder; it was almost the complete opposite. Back then I was trying to predominantly help myself, seeking money, cars, status, travel, reputation, all the stuff that comes with success, but now I genuinely wanted to help an organisation succeed. I wondered to myself when did that shift occur, and why?

"So you are looking at this job for the right reasons, and you don't desperately need the job. That's a good position to be in; you will perform better in the interview as a result. You can be open and honest and very direct, you can probably negotiate a little stronger as well. So why are you worrying about the interview? If you don't get it, you won't be shattered, and if you do it will be on your terms." As usual, Dave saw the situation clearly and in the right perspective.

"Maybe I am worrying unnecessarily about how I will present after being out of it for a while. You're right there's nothing to worry about, cheers mate I better get going."

He was right; actually, I would be presenting my authentic self rather than trying to fit into their brief and specifications. It was a nice luxury. In fact, that's how we all should present ourselves in every situation, every time, drop the pretence and role-playing, be yourself and deal with the outcome when it happens. In this case, I didn't get the CEO role. But the Chairman and the Directors were impressed with my background and candour. And I must have demonstrated clearly to them what I could bring to the business because a couple of months later that they offered me a position on their Board when a vacancy was created. Which in hindsight I am enjoying far more than if I had the day to day stress of the being CEO.

12TH HOLE

Do we begin to care more about others naturally as we get a little older, or does experience teach us the benefits of being more considerate and compassionate and we just apply a learned behaviour? Nobody likes to see another player struggling on the course, and no matter how competitive we may be, most players will offer encouragement and support to their playing partners. It's a hollow victory to win because of another player's misfortune; you want to beat your opponents when they are at their best, and the pain of losing is lessened if you have given your best but have just been outplayed on the day. The sublime days are when everyone in the group plays well, and the praise and congratulations are heartfelt and genuine. It is a shared positive experience in an otherwise individual sport that feeds our growth as people and reinforces the purity of this game.

The Players Championship at TPC Sawgrass Stadium Course is regarded as the fifth major, and the layout and the tournament are held in very high regard by players from all over the world. The spectators particularly appreciate the vantage points for viewing the action and how the finishing holes regularly produce a dramatic finish. The famous 17th hole provides entertainment throughout the tournament, even in practice rounds. Despite being a short hole that requires little more than a wedge or 9 iron, the unpredictable swirling wind and the island green creates pressure that can cause any player problems. A nice tradition has developed in the Wednesday practice round where caddies are challenged to hit a shot on this hole and try and win the annual nearest the pin prize. The prize is funded by the players who put $100 notes, generally in multiples, into a bucket on the tee, and the pool is shared between the winning caddy and the Bruce Edwards Foundation for ALS research. It regularly amounts to thousands of dollars. An additional perk is earned by the winning caddy; he is allocated a parking spot in the club car park for the week. The players enjoy swapping roles if only for one hole and will do their best caddy impersonations for that shot. It is quite a tough ask for the caddies. They have spent the day carrying a heavy bag around, haven't hit a single shot so far and sometimes haven't even played for weeks. And they are then thrust onto one of the most daunting stages in front of the cameras, and the crowds and are asked to hit a quality golf shot with a club that has specifications set up for a pro. Dave had participated in this fun event many times and always enjoyed it. This year he got to play it twice. His first shot using Rod's 9 iron found the water left. Rod and he were playing the practice round with Phil Mickelson. Phil's caddy Jim Mackay (Bones) is a solid player, and he hit his shot on the green, but as a right-hander, he had to use one of Rod's clubs. Phil's shot flew over the green and found the water, so there was a lot of good-natured ribbing from the rest of the group. Phil is well known for liking a contest and a wager, so he challenged them all. The right-handed players, Rod, Bones, and Dave all had to hit with one of Phil's left-handed clubs, and he would use one of Rod's. Phil went first and hit it on the front of the green.

"Guess I've been playing on the wrong side of the ball all these years." He joked.

Rod's attempt came up woefully short. Bones made a better pass at it but hit the edge of the green, and it came back in the water. Phil was beaming anticipating cleaning up on the bet. Dave stepped up, and without a practice swing hit it to 10 feet, well inside Phil's effort. The cash changed hands, and they all walked forward to the green laughing. Rod was still enjoying acting as Dave's caddy and was carrying the bag along the edge of the water, he came up beside Dave and said,

"Don't suppose you're going to tell him that you're a natural left-hander?"

"They call me Billy not silly!" Dave replied with a satisfied grin.

Rod made the cut comfortably and was within striking distance of the leaders. He had played well but not great. Dave could sense his stress levels were a little elevated; he probably feared another weekend not quite getting into contention on Sunday afternoon. Dave asked him about his dinner plans because he knew the family hadn't made this trip as they had some visitors at home for the weekend.

"You know I just don't feel like going to any of the restaurants around here tonight. They're full of players and industry people. I'm not in the mood to talk about golf and the tour issues tonight. I might get something in my room." His tone of voice concerned Dave; this wasn't the mental state of a potential winner. He had an idea.

"Tell you what Rod I don't think it's a good thing to sit around on your own tonight. Let me show you somewhere you wouldn't expect. The change of pace might give you a boost." Rod started to protest, but Dave insisted. "Just trust me on this, go and grab a shower, throw some jeans on and I'll swing by for you in about an hour."

Rod had been following Dave for about 15 mins, and his initial thought that he was being taken to a quiet restaurant that Dave liked had now been replaced by a concern that it may be some kind of a prank. They had started out across the carpark, past the equipment trailers, and passed through the lot for the motorhomes that a few of the players prefer to flying to each event and staying in hotels all the time. He was a little relieved that they walked straight through quickly because he was worried Dave might have organised to visit one of those players and their family. Finally, they came to an area behind the practice range that was only lit by flickering firelight. There were a few tarps up and a couple of tents. He could smell smoke, and the unmistakable aroma of southern spiced BBQ suddenly made him feel hungry. There was a low murmur of voices and the occasional raucous laugh. About a dozen guys were sitting around the fire and drinking beers out of an esky full of ice. The esky looked suspiciously like the ones that were on each tee with water and sports drinks for the players. As they came around the hedge, one of the men sitting around the fire recognised Dave instantly and jumped up, greeting him warmly.

"Hey Davey, it's been a while buddy come and have a beer, who's this with you?"

"Way too long, this is a good mate of mine from Sydney; Rod say g'day to Allen Johnson."

"Ah another Aussie I see, hi Rod, welcome to the

smokehouse, we used to get together at events just to drink and smoke cigars, but now we seem to mostly smoke Rib joints. Hey, Tommy are you keeping an eye on those ribs?" Al shouted across Rod to the guy closest to the BBQ, and he got a happy thumbs up from Tommy.

"So Rod who's bag are you on this week?" Al had assumed that Rod was also a caddy and Rod glanced apprehensively at Dave, who quickly pulled Al aside and said quietly,

"Actually Al, Rod is playing in the tournament, I'm on his bag, but can we keep it between just us, we are looking for some low key relaxation tonight. There aren't any other caddies here are there?"

"Gotcha, I understand, no there's just us sweat hogs here tonight."

Dave explained later to Rod that these guys erected and dismantled all the tents and stands each week and some of the caddies knew about the "smokehouse" and would come along for a cheap meal and some laughs in return for a carton of beer or a bottle of bourbon. These men worked exceptionally hard before and after the tournament, but during the week they were only required for maintenance or emergency jobs, so mid-tournament was like their weekend. It was backbreaking work in all kinds of weather, and all for a flat hourly rate and a meal allowance and next week, they would do it all over again in another city. They had worked out long ago that if they cooked for themselves, they could pocket most of their meal allowances, and if a few caddies turned up with some drinks then even better! Now Rod understood why Dave was carrying a small bag. He handed over the entry fee, a large bottle of Jack Daniels and two bottles of Australian Shiraz.

"Yes sir!" exclaimed Al loudly as he accepted the bounty.

"Make some room guys for my Aussie pals."

Rod and Dave enjoyed a great night with the sweat hogs; they were in fits of laughter trying to understand some of the Australian sayings that Dave was attempting to explain. When he introduced "fair suck of the sav" Tommy nearly choked on his corn, as Dave tried valiantly to elaborate the meaning, it only got worse. What a terrific bunch of guys, they all worked so hard and weren't paid all that much, but they were the happiest group of blokes that Rod had seen for quite a while. He had noticed early on that Al had a prosthetic leg. During the night Al told him that he was working on a circus tent years ago and he fell about thirty feet and badly smashed his leg, and it couldn't be saved. He had tried to seek compensation for his injuries from the owners of the circus. Their response was to fire him and not long after that they went out of business, so he had no chance of pursuing any payment. Still, he didn't appear to hold any grudges; he just got on with life. Dave didn't meet Al until after the accident, but they had become great mates. It was Dave who sourced the latest prosthetic for him through a contact he has back in Australia in a company doing remarkable work in the field. Al didn't say, but he gave Rod the impression that Dave had also paid for it. Meeting these men and hearing about their lives made Rod think hard about his own blessings. He thanked Al and the boys warmly for their hospitality and company and made a genuine promise to come back again, plus he made a mental note to send them a case of wine at every tournament he played in from now on.

As they walked back to the hotel, Rod thanked Dave. It was just the tonic he needed.

"No problem, that's my job." But Rod didn't think for a second that this was part of the job description. The way Davey looked out for other people and was able to make so many positive changes to their lives was amazing. That he never wanted to take any credit or acknowledgement was the most impressive feature, he just quietly went about it as if it was his purpose in life. To use another Australian aphorism, Rod thought to himself,

"This guy is a bloody legend."

The next day Rod felt refreshed and excited about the round ahead. He hadn't been so relaxed on the course for ages. They walked onto the 17th tee having just birdied sixteen to be 4 under for the day. As he looked across the water to the green, for the first time, he took notice of the grandstands and nearby marquees and thought about Al and the team building them. As if he could read Rod's mind Dave pondered out loud,

"I wonder how long it takes to pull them all down." As they both pictured the process Rod imagined the guys clamouring up and down the structure, straining with the physical effort and battling the wind, he could hear the yelling and Al's loud laugh. Suddenly, popping a wedge onto a green in relatively calm conditions seemed comparatively simple. Dave handed him the pitching wedge saying,

"134 yards, breeze off the right, your line is the left edge of the bunker; the slope should bring it back down to the pin."

He hit it right on the line Dave wanted, and it rolled to about four feet. He was never going to miss the putt. A safe par at the last and a round of 67 put him two shots behind the leader, and he would be playing in the penultimate group in the final round.

Many people reach their forties having lived much the same way since early adulthood, focused on their own needs and wants, building a career and nurturing their growing family. Single-mindedness and self-interest are needed to achieve the socially accepted standard of lifestyle advertised by everything and everybody around us. The ubiquitous messaging can make it difficult to distinguish between encouragement and conformity. There are cultural, economic, technological and legal guidelines and boundaries that we must work within. Yet at this stage of life it is common to start questioning why we are doing certain things, or at the very least challenge how we are going about it. We may retain the same goals but now choose to try different methods and pathways to get there. Two thirds of the way through a round of golf, we reach a similar point where we might start experimenting with shot or club choices. We realise that something we have been attempting over and over is not working on this day, or we recall a suggestion from a lesson or an article we have read. If it has been a lousy round so far, we can even reject our game plan or changes our coach has suggested and employ a radical approach. It always happens around the first few holes of the back nine, but every now and then it works.

Dave had been studying the vital holes on the course all week, tabulating Rod's results and observing his playing partners and evaluating their strategies versus their performances. Most commentators and players believe the last few holes especially 16, 17 and 18 are the key holes, especially on Sunday, and it is crucial to play them well to post a good score, but that can be said about the finishing stretch on any championship course. There are very few easy finishes in the premier events on tour. Dave had concluded that it is even more important how you build your run into the last stages of the round. What has happened earlier on the back nine can affect your state of mind. If you have stumbled the tendency is to play aggressively to make up the difference, and a player will take too many risks. If you have built a healthy lead often then a player will play safe and try and protect their score. On this course, the holes around the turn offer up some good birdie chances, and if the player takes advantage of these opportunities, this will provide useful momentum for the rest of the round. In the four holes from 9 through 12, there are two par fives and two par fours. All can be birdied. Dave had observed that depending on the wind direction, most players attempted to reach the ninth and the eleventh in two shots to have a chance at eagle. He did some research to add to his personal knowledge from caddying here the last few years, and found some surprising stats. He asked Rod to meet him for a quiet coffee before they went to the range.

"Rod I've been studying how you and the other guys have played this course, and I've also looked up some statistics. I firmly believe that the key to winning here is taking advantage of holes 9 thru 12, and then playing solidly the last six holes without needing to push too hard. You and most of the other guys try to reach 9 and 11 in two, except if you miss the fairway or the wind is hurting, but surprisingly, you make birdie more often when you are forced to lay up than when you go for the green. I found some data, since 2003 63.6% of players have gone for the green on the 11th but only 12.4% have hit the green. I know why they go for the green because the surrounding bunker provides a safety net, or so they believe, but playing from that bunker isn't always straightforward."

"So what are you suggesting Dave?" Rod asked with a concerned look that suggested he might not like what was coming.

"I want you to lay up on the last three par fives, including the 16th, and on 11 I want you to hit 3 wood and then two pitching wedges," Rod said nothing initially and drank his coffee slowly. He knew from experience that he could trust his caddy's intuition, but he needed a little more convincing this time.

"Davey, Justin is ahead of me on the leaderboard, you know he will go for every par five in two, if he makes eagle I won't be able to catch him."

"Don't worry he'll make par on all the par fives today." Dave said matter of factly.

"How do you know that?" Rod said incredulously.

"I can't explain how I know it, but sometimes I just do. Let's get to the practice range."

Both players were square for the tournament after nine holes; Rod birdied the 9th and the 11th holes after laying up and birdied the 12th after a beautiful approach shot. Justin birdied 12 and 13, and they were even again. Things got a little tense on 16 when after laying up as per Dave's recommendation Rod failed to birdie the par 5 and believed he had handed the trophy to his opponent who he was sure would birdie 16 behind him. Rod played a solid shot to the island green 17th, and as they were walking to the green they heard a loud groan from the crowd and looked back to see Justin with his hands on his head, he had missed a four-footer for birdie. Just as Dave had predicted, Justin failed to birdie any of the par fives today. Rod's twenty foot put slowly trickled across the slope and with its last roll fell in the side of the cup. The crowd roared, and Justin saw and heard it all from back on the tee. Perhaps the atmosphere affected his concentration because he barely kept his ball on the green and he did well to make par. Rod was fuelled by adrenalin and smoked his three wood nearly 300 yards down the 18th fairway. Dave slowed him up after he started to race ahead to the ball. He talked about the other night at the smokehouse to distract him and settle him down. Once at the ball Rod wanted to go for the pin, he was still worried that Justin could birdie the last.

"The middle of the green is all you need Rod." Dave calmly reassured him. Rod two-putted for par and walked off to the scorers hut mentally spent. He glanced down the fairway and saw Justin in the right rough, hard to make birdie from there he thought to himself, and it proved to be, Justin made par and Rod was the Players Champion. He came out of the hut to the cheers and well wishes from the crowd and some of the other players, as he walked around the corner, he felt her before he saw her. Donna was here to share this moment with him. They embraced for what seemed like a full five minutes, and he could only manage one word through the tears,

"How?"

"I think you can guess sweetheart." Donna whispered to him, pushing his face tenderly to the right, so he was looking across at Dave who was packing up the gear.

The next thirty minutes were a blur of interviews and handshakes and then suddenly it was time to accept the trophy and say a few words. Rod thanked his family and supporters plus the usual list of people who support and manage the tournament. When he thanked Dave, he got a little choked up but was able to get out how much his caddy meant to him. Right at the end of his speech he sent out special thanks to the guys from the smokehouse. He said the time they spent together the other night lifted his spirits and made him appreciate all the unseen work done by the hundreds of men and women who make each tournament happen. He told everyone there and those watching on TV that the world of golf depends on crews like this and how it had restored his faith in people and the future and gave him the focus he needed to win this week. He then urged every player to shout them a beer. He walked off with the trophy to wild applause and laughter.

Al and some of the smokehouse guys were watching the

presentation on a monitor in one of the tents they were about to strip down. Tommy came up to Al saying,

"Shit Al, I didn't know he was a golfer. I was telling him the other night that some of the tour players are spoilt prima donnas!!" Al put his arm around his shoulders and said,

"A few might be Tommy, but not this guy."

13ᵀᴴ HOLE

The concept of patience is frequently discussed in the game of golf. Players speak in clichés about it in pre-round interviews and post-round press conferences, using well-rehearsed phrasing so often that it gets repetitive and the importance of what they are saying is lost in the overuse of the language. Announcers reference it so frequently it becomes white noise. However, applying patience to your game plan and returning to that mindset as often as possible during a round is extremely useful, the practice itself being far more beneficial than the redundant commentary. Like many things in life, if you let it come to you and don't chase it then your expectations match your results more often, plus you expend less energy in the process! It takes a little while and multiple mistakes for most of us to learn this, some never do.

There's a stage of life when a substantial proportion of people resign themselves to "settling." They just accept what they have and how they are living and end up miserable and merely exist unhappily. They may work in a job they hate, or endure an unhappy relationship. Some will suffer poor health or fitness, or live all their life with lost dreams and regrets. A sad fraction may simply be lonely, overwhelmed or have lost direction. This world can sometimes seem like a constant trade-off, and the currency is happiness. Similarly, some golfers will tell themselves they are always unlucky and get more bad breaks than everyone else, and others who believe they can never improve their weaknesses and trudge around the course week after week frustrated and mentally beaten up. I have spoken earlier in this book about players needing to find their optimum performance level and realistically work towards that. But patiently finding your level is very different to passively accepting your current situation and letting that determine how you have to live or play. There is always something that you can change. Take the golfer who firmly believes they get more than their share of bad luck. Instead of complaining about the terrible lies they keep getting in bunkers, they could change their strategy or shot choices, so they are in fewer bunkers. If they consistently spray their tee shots into the trees and put themselves in unplayable lies, they could give themselves less grief and stress if they hit it in the fairway more often. They need to develop a go-to shot that they can rely on to help them hit the fairway when they are playing tight holes. It's an easier game from the fairway and players are generally luckier playing from the short grass! The luck of the bounce will always play a part in golf, but the good and bad bounces tend to even themselves out over time so reducing the risks can only improve that ratio and our enjoyment of the game. Be patient and believe that good breaks must eventually come to you.

Dave taught me a valuable lesson about belief a few years ago. I was exhibiting my own version of lack of patience on the course and voicing my frustration in the clubhouse after another disappointing round. My game was on a downward trend, and so every time I went to the course I was getting anxious even before I started playing. I was forlornly hoping that each round would be the start of some improved form and if I began poorly, I could feel myself getting tense and angry quickly. I knew that like most golfers, my good rounds tended to come in bunches and I would enjoy a string of good scores and when I eventually lost form it then took some time to return. I was trying to force the start of my upward swing.

"You seemed a little tense out there today Dougal; you lost your composure after the first bad shot on the second hole." Dave opened the conversation as he put a couple of beers on the table.

"I know mate, sorry it's just been getting to me a bit lately, and I just can't seem to put a good round together. I have no consistency, and I can't get a break, I seem to get every bad lie or bounce going. Maybe I'm just getting old."

"You know Bernhard Langer is 7 years older than you and Freddie Couples has got you by a year, and before you say they're pros, I'm 5 years older than you are, and I kicked your backside today! I don't think it's an age thing" Dave in his usual manner inflected this statement with a serious pitch, so it sounded like an invitation to respond.

"What is it then?" There was enough annoyance in my voice to put that knowing half-smile on Davey's face that I know so well. That expression always preceded a pearl of wisdom or a piece of valuable advice, and as dispirited as I was I was keen to hear it.

"What were you expecting out there today?"

"I don't know, to find some form maybe, hit some solid shots." I said glumly.

"And what did you believe was going to happen?" Dave quietly asked.

"I just told you!"

"They're not the same things." He said it as if I should know the difference, but he continued.

"Having an expectation is ok, but it can often be just hopefulness, or a wish, maybe an educated estimate. There isn't the certainty or conviction that can make things happen seemingly by sheer willpower. Belief has a power of its own often flying in the face of accepted knowledge, past performance or the consensus of those around you. Believing you can do something changes your state of mind and influences your actions. The chances of succeeding are much higher if you possess an unshakeable belief that you can do it. But it works the other way too, believe you can't, and you won't. So I ask you again what did you believe was going to happen today?"

I thought about it for a minute or two and then said,

"To be honest Davey, I believed I would play poorly again, but I was hoping I wouldn't."

"And guess what, you were right. You are a self-fulfilling prophecy. I've seen players on tour do some amazing things that to everyone else seemed improbable. And yet you got the sense from their body language and expression that they just knew they could do it. Do you ever wonder why certain players can continually perform incredible feats under pressure at precisely the right moments?"

"Talent and experience I suppose." Even as I said these words, I knew it was a weak answer.

"Every single player on tour has talent, and drive, and years of experience. They aren't out on tour by accident, there are no overnight successes. These guys have had highly successful amateur and junior careers, and they all work incredibly hard. But like many sports, the very top echelons of players always seem to be able to deliver when it counts. They believe Dougal; deep down they know that it's their purpose, their destiny. It's a force within them that they have somehow harnessed. I swear that sometimes it's palpable; you can feel it as they walk past you and as you observe them applying that belief there is an eerie calmness around them, it's quite something to experience from close proximity. But it's in all of us to some degree. I'm sure you have completely believed something was going to happen for you in the past, and you orientate your thinking and behaviours to the end goal, and magically it comes off, often with surprising ease. Now, the sermon is over, and I believe it's your shout." He finished with a grin.

I wasn't ready to end the discussion yet; he had got my attention.

"How do you get that belief, Davey?"

"Now that is the crucial question, and I want you to think about the answer for a while. If I gave you a simple answer it would be wrong because it would be my answer, you have to find your own, and the only way is to go through the process yourself, now how about that beer?"

We didn't speak about patience and belief any further in the clubhouse. After the presentation, we left together about an hour later. As we walked to the carpark out of the blue Davey says to me,

"Mahatma Gandhi had a great saying; he said Man

becomes what he believes himself to be. Self-belief is everything Dougal, and the most important part is maintaining your fundamental confidence in your abilities irrespective of your performances. So many variables can influence your scores, but you have to believe you are a good player. You had 2 birdies today, but overall your score disappointed you. How often do you play and not have a single birdie?"

"Rarely." My answer was short because I was still processing the fact that Dave reads and quotes Mahatma Gandhi's words! He continued to that point.

"And you probably play twice a week, so that's 100 rounds a year having 1 or two birdies most rounds and sometimes 3 or 4 or even more on a good day. So let's say that you make between 200 and 300 birdies in a year and throw in a few eagles as well. Self-efficacy is the belief in your own ability to perform in specific situations and accomplish certain tasks. I want you to believe that you are a good enough player that throughout each year no matter how you score, you know that you will make hundreds of birdies. That certainty will boost your confidence which shapes your self-belief. There are guys behind us in the clubhouse who wouldn't make 300 birdies in their lifetime."

This was quite profound stuff from Davey, and it had me listening intently.

"Now I want you to think all week that you are a skilled player, confidence can be learned and developed, but at the

14TH HOLE

Your mid-fifties is a significant and transitional time of life. You have the sobering awareness and the evidence that physically you are past your best. What has happened in your life and the decisions you've made have brought you to this point. But it is easy to gloss over your successes and only focus on the regrets. You fear that time may be running out to realise your dreams, repair mistakes and setbacks and if you allow it, there can be a devastating effect on your psyche. But there are always people who revel in this life stage and say it is the best time of their life. They are comfortable where they are and who they are. It is all about perspective. Likewise, on the golf course, you can be walking down the 14th fairway, fuming at what has occurred so far, you can be in a desolate depression or happily bouncing along energised and enthusiastic if it

*has been a successful round. Though with some
people even if the golf has been a disaster, the
day has still been a triumph. Perspective... what
you look for, what you see, and what you take
forward from each situation is reflected back in
the future.*

A friend of mine, Edmund, was playing with Dave
recently. Dave is extremely fastidious with the fitting
and set up of players' equipment. Edmund had been
an excellent player for a long time, but in recent months
his game had been deteriorating, especially his driving
and long iron play. He was frustrated and depressed and
was vocalising his misery all the way around the course
that day. Dave had worked out the problem on the second
hole. What was interesting was Edmund had already been
given the answer multiple times by teachers and equipment
salespeople. They had even shown him clear, unquestionable
data from their monitors, but Edmund stubbornly believed
that he still needed to play with stiff shafts; he was a low
marker after all and feared losing control with a softer shaft.
Well at least that was the way he rationalised it. Dave knew
Edmund took great pride in his physical fitness and still did
a lot of running and cycling at the age of 58. Using a scenario
he knew would align with Edmund's interest in athletics he
asked a simple question.

"Edmund can you still run as fast as you did at 21?"

"Of course not Dave" Edmund replied with an accompanying lift of one eyebrow.

"Then what makes you think you can swing a golf club as fast as you did 20 or 30 years ago?"

The logic was incontrovertible; this short exchange happened on the 17th tee, Edmund didn't speak a word again until they went into the clubhouse and even then it was a very stilted and restrained conversation. Dave could feel the conflict Edmund was experiencing between his ego and reality. As he was leaving to go home that afternoon, he left him with one last thought,

"Remember, the stickers on golf shafts are removable!" The next week Edmund was fitted for regular shafts, his game improved remarkably, and now he happily tells that story to everyone he plays with, normally after he hits a pure drive straight down the middle. As Dave says, you don't write your club specifications on the scorecard, but what you do write down is significantly influenced by them.

Irrespective of what has happened so far, and wherever and whenever you may be there is always a new target to set, new tools to use and improvement to gain. Looking is more than just seeing, it is about finding...

Dave worked steadily on various tours for nearly two decades and the success he achieved, especially during his tenure with Rod Hazelbrook, gave him quite a high profile, and he was continually in demand. There were always offers coming in, and some were incredibly tempting financially, but Dave was very disciplined about how he evaluated each one. His upbringing and deeply entrenched moral standards were his trusted compasses. The money on offer was barely a consideration. He believed that if he took on a job for the right reasons, one that was compatible with his values and consistent with his ambitions and sense of purpose, then the remuneration would take care of itself. He also felt strongly that the integrity of this game warranted the application of a moral code that regulated all activities across the whole spectrum of the golf industry even if it was only self-regulation. In his mind, this meant both personal behaviour and commercial dealings. Sadly, despite the game of golf being unequalled by any other sport for integrity and sportsmanship, there were still individuals who strayed into the murky waters of self-interest, self-importance and ego-driven behaviour. And even when realising their predicament, some stubbornly refused to ask for help to navigate their return, and a few never made it back at all. The stories vary from players changing equipment for large endorsement payments and ruining their game, to questionable business deals, gambling and substance addictions, dreadfully handled caddy, manager or coach sackings, and high profile relationship breakdowns and infidelity. All the usual human peccadillos and not unique to golf, but the telling observation is that in most cases once a player was involved in these type of problems and scandals, there were negative consequences, particularly for their performances and results. Not that surprising with all the distractions and media attention but it seems more pronounced in golf than in other fields. Davey theorises that the game of golf is so challenging to play at the highest level. And it has such an entrenched legacy of self-imposed values, that if an individual is bestowed with the natural gifts to excel at the game, and they disrespect that and transgress in any way, then some higher power takes those gifts away or at least reduces their ability from the rarefied level they previously enjoyed.

"I'll guarantee you $150k per year as a retainer, plus the usual 10% of winnings, and 15% if I win a major. You can travel with me in my plane, so your travel costs are reduced, but accommodation is your responsibility. I need an answer by tonight".

Davey was standing outside the Callaway equipment trailer listening with surprise to this offer from Ronson Oliver-Keeley, or ROK as he liked people to call him. An up and coming player who had captured the media and public attention with his aggressive playing style and brash confidence, ROK was contracted to Callaway and so was Rod Hazelbrook, so Dave knew him and had been paired with him a few times. There was no denying his talent, but his style was one that Dave felt was bad for the game's future and the wrong type of influence on kids taking up the game. Being ambushed like this annoyed Dave especially as it felt like a rushed afterthought as they crossed paths at the trailer. A meaningful discussion about changing players surely warranted a more formal and planned meeting over a drink or dinner, or at least in a hotel room in private not within earshot of about six guys in the trailer. Dave was there getting some adjustments done on Rod's irons when ROK had burst in through the door and threw his driver on the bench proclaiming it to be crap and demanded a few more to trial. He also didn't like the reference to ROK winning a major on his own. If he is going to pay 15% to his caddy isn't it a team effort, Dave reasoned, shouldn't it be "when WE win a major." Dave waited until ROK actually looked at him, while he was giving the offer he had been transfixed on his phone the whole time as if reading the details provided by someone else.

"ROK when did you fire Brian?" Brian was ROK's latest caddy.

"I haven't yet Dave, not until I find a replacement; we are just not getting the results we want."

I see Dave thought to himself, when you win a major you claim all the credit, but when you play poorly the caddy shares the blame. ROK continued,

"I heard that Rod was wimping out and going to play more on the Australian tour next year. That's practically a secondary tour, and the money is shit, so I thought you would be keen to pick up a bag on the US tour, you gotta look after yourself Dave?"

Quite a salesman young ROK, he now had insulted not only Rod as a player and a man but also the Australian tour despite both Dave and his player being Australians. Dave like everyone else knew that ROK's father was a high profile wealthy entertainment lawyer and guessed his privileged background and having grown up observing his father's hard-nosed work style glorified in the tabloids, had influenced his development and personality. He was also sure he had taken some direction from his father on how to pitch this offer.

"Why did you start playing golf ROK?" Dave asked in a matter of fact tone.

"Well I had scholarship offers for golf and basketball from UCLA and my father, and I felt that golf offered a much longer career option and earning potential especially from endorsement deals."

Dave said nothing for a short while, much in the way his father used to do when he was young. Then staring across the course as the sun was setting he said almost to himself,

"I love everything about this game, the values, the challenge, the integrity, the variety, the scenery, the history, the competition and the relationships you develop at all levels. I consider myself one of the luckiest people on earth to do what I love for a living. I learn something new every day about the game, about people and most importantly about myself."

Dave turned and looked straight into ROK's eyes with an intensity that made ROK take half a step backward

"So that you know, Rod is playing closer to home this year because his father is very sick. Even if he doesn't play a single tournament, I'll be there with him. Good luck with your search for a new caddy."

As Dave started to walk away, he noticed the technicians were all at the windows of the Callaway trailer. Brett Williams, their head of tour operations, nodded approvingly and gave him a thumbs up.

15ᵀᴴ HOLE

By the time we have reached our sixties inevitably, we will have all experienced loss. When you are confronted with loss or near loss, the fear of an empty space that can never be wholly filled can cause profound changes in your perspectives. You are fortunate if it is a wakeup call and you get a second chance, but if not there is still the opportunity to gain something from a painful and gut-wrenching experience. The losses you can experience on the golf course pale by comparison, but there are still plenty to overcome by late in the round. You may have given back the gains from a good start, lost confidence in your ability to play certain shots that day, lost your focus, gone off your game plan or even lost your composure. As hard as it appears at the time, there are always lessons to learn, new skills to hone and advantages to gain. Humans possess a unique adaptability. We not only adapt to our environment but we can adapt our environment to meet our needs and desires. However, the golfer's psychology and subsequent behaviours are often stuck in a repetitive loop.

"How would you act on the course if you knew that it was going to be your very last game of golf ever?" A loaded question if ever there was one. Davey had endured my frustration and grumpiness all day, and as we went up the last fairway, he dropped this on me.

"Point taken, apologies mate I know I wasn't the best company today," I said uncomfortably.

"It's not that so much, I just recalled how you were a few years back. You had been really crook for a couple of months, and then you had to have that emergency surgery. I remember seeing you in the hospital, and all you talked about was getting back out on the course. You were concerned that you might not be able to do so."

"Yeah, that wasn't a fun time." I replied, Dave continued,

"When you came back to golf, which I thought was a little too early by the way, you were still very weak, but you couldn't have cared less about your score or how you hit the ball, you were just over the moon to be back. Nothing bothered you during the game. If you missed a short putt or hit it sideways, you simply laughed it off. Now you're back to full health, and every bad shot or bounce grinds you into a deep despair."

"That was a little different though." I said defensively.

"Not really, let's suppose something happens to you tonight or even on the drive home, is that how you would have wanted to say goodbye to golf, to this game you love so much? When you were sick I know it was a shithouse time, it was for all of us, but what a great lesson we were given about appreciating the best things in life and golf is one of them. I'm as guilty as you, I've forgotten as well, and I also lose my temper on the course sometimes. To see you so unhappy out there today made me think. When you were busting your stitches post-surgery trying to swing, and you couldn't break ninety, it was the happiest I have ever seen you playing golf."

I thought a lot about what Davey had said to me for days. He was right of course, he nearly always is, and his ability to observe situations and find the real meaning was highly developed. It's true if you somehow mysteriously knew that it was the last round you were ever going to play, you would enjoy every shot, be more aware of each sensation savouring the feel of the club in your hands, the ground under your feet and the impact of the ball, you'd notice and appreciate the whole vista all day down to the smallest leaf or creature. You would try to store and file every memory. Your actual score would be immaterial and almost irrelevant. In fact, I suppose if it were your last round you would want to hit as many shots as possible, not less. Plus the irony is that when you aren't stressing about your results as much, you invariably have your best scores. There's a song by Tim McGrath called "Live like you were Dying," which tells the story of a man who after getting a terminal diagnosis, started living the life he had always wanted to and became the type of person he should have been. This chat with Dave provided me a similar revelation.

In professional golf as a player moves through their career there are constant changes and challenges. Like all of us, physical abilities will diminish, ageing is something that none of us can defeat or avoid. There is a counter balance though, as we lose some of our athletic ability, experience and shrewdness can be applied to offset the loss. Not everyone manages it though. Even with the advancement in technology, nobody can continue to overpower golf courses forever. The canny players accept the loss of distance and the ability to hit the ball high, compressing the ball to generate extremely high spin. They will look for other ways to work their way around a course. That is one of the great positives of golf; there are so many different ways to post a score. A great example is the Spaniard Miguel Angel Jiménez. Now into his fifties, he is still very competitive on the main tour against the young guns and of course is one of the leading players on the senior tour. He has been playing with a patient cleverness for some years now. Fully accepting that he isn't going to match the length of the younger players, and so he plots his way around the course. Shaping his shots into tight pins, hitting low running draws off the tee to get every yard out of his drives, using his short game skills and exhibiting an obvious belief in his ability to do so. The most admirable part of Miguel's game is his attitude. You can tell that he absolutely loves being out on tour, he enjoys the perks but is still grateful for the lifestyle it has afforded him. You never see him losing his temper after a bad shot or getting stressed if he is outdriven by 50 yards by players 30 years his junior. He is thankful he is still walking the fairways with them. He enjoys his cigars, great wine, and good food but is very serious about keeping his game sharp, but equally, he has the right perspective. Golf is a game, a great game that is his livelihood, but it is an activity that should be pleasurable, and he doesn't hide his delight, why should he? He is so enigmatic and refreshing that it's no wonder he has been called the most interesting man in golf.

Augusta in April 1996 was when Greg Norman suffered his worst loss, and his pain and humiliation were acutely on public exhibition, opening him up to ridicule. After playing brilliantly for three days and creating a six-shot lead going into the last round of the US Masters, including posting a record-equalling 63 in the first round, very few people would have begrudged him the trophy he had coveted the most.

He had endured more than his share of heartbreaking near misses at this place, a course and championship that he loved. Practically everyone had conceded him victory, everyone that was except Nick Faldo. Something was different that Sunday, his tempo, his demeanour and swing were all different to what he had shown for the prior three days. There has been a massive amount of speculation and analysis about what happened to Greg, including the suggestion that if he had been playing with anyone else on that day, he might have continued his confident run to the green jacket. I don't want to add to the long list of commentary about what happened and why. I am interested in the aftermath, and what Greg gained from such an otherwise crushing loss. The way he handled such a defeat and how he bravely and honestly presented himself to the world's media I believe enhanced his reputation and earned him respect for something other than his golfing prowess. He showed his character and opened up about his feelings. That takes strength, and as a result, people weren't only sorry for him, they had admiration. The other positive was he and Faldo shared a moment that created a connection that had been missing in the past, they had both stated before that they were never really friendly as they fought for years for the world number one position in golf. Their styles and personalities were in direct contrast. To Faldo's credit, he initiated it by embracing Norman on the last green and giving him private words of encouragement, which

Greg duly acknowledged in subsequent press conferences. The point is that while of course Greg Norman would have preferred to win the US Masters, and he lost an opportunity that he regrettably never converted for the rest of his career, he also gained from the experience as well. If he had won, we might have never seen the parts of his soul that he bared to us that emotional evening, and we certainly wouldn't have heard about the compassionate side of Faldo's character that everyone assumed was non-existent. How gracious a winner can be and how noble a loser should be, were both on display that day.

Sometimes how you carry the yearning for that which you can never hold is far more revealing and lasting than the nonchalant pageantry of showing off your easily won prize.

16ᵀᴴ HOLE

The 16ᵗʰ hole in a round can feel like turning into the home straight in a race. Where you are placed in the race and how you are feeling will influence the choices you make and the strategy you apply for the finishing stretch. Paradoxically you may even choose not to use any strategy just when you need it the most. Discovery is sometimes deliberate but often random. The unexpected discoveries are the ones that can affect the most profound changes because unlike the deliberate discovery which is limited to a narrow field of planned search, the discoveries that surprise you the most can move you in directions and distances you could never have anticipated. A shock can be exhilarating or distressing but it comes with an intrinsic power that stuns you into action. If you hole a miraculous shot or make a ridiculous error in golf, or you encounter a life-changing

event, you will react, you must. How and why
you respond either channels that power or makes
you lose control of it.

Two events occurred within a week of each other which were at the time seemingly unrelated. When I realised the connection between them, my life changed forever. At a party to celebrate my 48th birthday I was convinced by my sister to go and visit a clairvoyant she had seen a few times in recent years. Naturally sceptical of such people I was amazed at how readily I agreed. I put it down to two things, the sincerity of my sister's motives and that I had been through a rough year personally, so partly out of respect for her and my own jaded curiosity I took the card, and the next day made the appointment. That I was asked to attend a remote caravan park at 11:30 pm was a little alarming, but a few days later I pulled into the carpark on a night so dark that the streetlights around the entrance to the caravan park barely made any difference to the gloom. I pulled my collar up to keep the icy penetrating rain off my neck and ran across to the awning attached to the second caravan on the left. Once inside I saw three other people waiting their turn to see the clairvoyant Carmen. The décor inside this tent was as you would expect, a mixture of gypsy styled furnishings and tapestries, punctuated with an assortment of new age artefacts. No one said a word, they sat there absorbed in their own world, and it struck me that by their demeanour they all were living with a heavy burden of some kind. The last person to go in before me was dressed in business clothes and carried a briefcase. He was called in from the other room by name. This was how Carmen ushered each person in; I had still not laid eyes on her. The man entered, and within a couple of minutes, I heard the distinct sound of the briefcase latches opening. A few minutes later he exited, ashen-faced in a definite hurry and left without even a glance in my direction. My mind was whirling with possible reasons for his meeting and his urgent exit when I heard my name called,

"Doug, please come in."

Carmen was younger than I had expected but dressed in a way that gave her the appearance of someone much older, and she projected a bleak world-weary resignation. She began with the typical questions and statements and right at the point when I started to think it was the worst $50 I had ever spent and was considering leaving, Carmen's tone of voice changed and the expression on her face intensified, and she said to me,

"You have someone around you who has passed. He passed over very young, very quickly and quite violently. This man is always around you and is watching over you, and he has a strong and close connection with you, do you have any idea who this may be?"

I honestly didn't, and I said so. Then I noticed Carmen

began moaning slightly and running her hand across her neck repeatedly, and she said with what appeared to be some discomfort,

"I am getting an awful feeling in my neck, right here," and she dragged her hand in a cutting motion from ear to ear. Again she questioned me,

"Are you sure you can't think of who this might be?"

I said I didn't have any clue. Carmen went on to describe this man and some of his habits and told me that he was my guide and my guardian, but it still meant nothing to me. I left the reading startled at what I had heard but not overly concerned because at that point I didn't believe anything she said.

A few days later I was at my parents for dinner, my sister was also coming, and I couldn't wait to tell her what I thought of her clairvoyant, but I was there first so I thought I would share the episode with Mum. I relayed what had happened with half a smile, rolling my eyes and my mother looked up at me with an expression on her face that I had never seen before. She said

"That is your great uncle Doug Nanfield, and we named you after him. He was captured by the Japanese in WWII, and they executed him. They made him kneel down, and they cut his head off with a sword. He wasn't even 21 when it happened."

I was stunned. I had been told a few things about my

great uncle but had never heard the details of his death, and this is probably why I couldn't draw the connection when I was with Carmen, I honestly had no idea. When my sister arrived, I told her everything, but in a vastly different context than I had initially planned. I decided to try and find out everything I could about my great uncle Doug.

The following weekend I was fortunate to have been invited to a function to honour Dave and celebrate the success he has achieved as a caddy for the last couple of decades. He may have carried the bag, and a few players some will argue, all around the world, and had grown up in Victoria, but Queensland proudly claims him as one of our favourite sons, and Golf QLD was sponsoring this event. It was a great night and a fitting tribute to Dave. Near the end of the evening, one of his close mates from the tour read a short verse that he had found that he felt accurately represented the essence of Davey Neilson, and reflected the regard he is held in by those who know him and have worked with him. When I heard it, I couldn't have agreed more, so I asked for a copy to keep, the verse is below;

Character – The Unheralded Quality

Why is it that those who have fought the fiercest battles themselves, are often first to lend a hand without a moment of hesitation, and for others would step into the breach

This man is a friend admired and respected by all, a brother and son of the highest calibre, a mate with no peer

If you need help he is there, if you need a laugh he lightens the mood, he is the voice of reason giving you logical options for the conclusions you must reach

If you had to face adversity, you would want his strength and quality right beside you,

But before you noticed and without being asked, he would be in front of you taking each hit as your shield, that's what champions do...

The verse had a powerful impact on me, so I tried to search for its' origin. First I asked his mate who found it. He said that he just looked for inspirational verses on the internet and he liked this one the best. There wasn't even a listing of who wrote it, just an obscure index number. I spent weeks researching it, and after a few dead ends, I got a tip from the lady at the library that it may be in some of the old military texts because of the unique indexing. After two afternoons in that library fruitlessly scrolling through page after page of their database, I had found nothing. I was ready to abandon my search when finally a page opened with a series of poems written by soldiers in that theatre of war. A short scan through them and I found the verse I was looking for, and I was relieved to see the authors' name and the background to the story. The first time I read it my head started to spin, I couldn't believe what was in front of me. I read it twice more until it had sunk in. The man who wrote the poem was a private John Brooker. He wrote it for a mate of his who had gone missing in the Parit Sulong Massacre in Malaysia on the 21st January 1942. When I read the final line from a copy of an official service and casualty form my heart nearly leapt out of my chest.

Private Doug Nanfield NX 7072 – "Became missing on 22/1/42 at the Battle of Muar and for official purposes is presumed to be dead." – PARIT SULONG

The verse read out for Davey was written about my great uncle Doug, who Carmen insists is with me now and looking out for me.

I don't remember driving home from the library that day, but I can still summon how I felt. My mind was racing, and I was shocked but in a strange way excited about this revelation. I couldn't help myself from trying to see a connection with Davey and what he has meant to me and how he has helped me. I had so many questions that most likely had no plausible or logical answers. If I dared to entertain the idea that it was possible for someone to influence your life from an unseen and non-living dimension, could my great uncle be using

Davey as that instrument? Do the incredible insights, and the knack he has of seemingly knowing what is going to happen and the judgment and vision he displays, all preternaturally come from somewhere else? It sounds ridiculous and far-fetched, and even more so now as I write it down, but I wanted so badly for it to be true.

I began looking for parallels, no matter how spurious they sounded, for example, I even noted that they have the same initials, and they were both left-handed. It's interesting when you want something to be real, and it is incredibly important to you, how easy it is to make leaps of faith beyond your normal level of tolerance and accepted knowledge. Your paradigms adjust to your emotions and your desires. The unusual coexistence of blindness to repudiation and a newly enhanced way of seeing things energises your soul.

I was quietly sitting with an excellent glass of red, just mulling over my recent discoveries and trying vainly to organise them into some logical pattern. The phone startled me out of my reflection.

"Dougal I saw John Hanwood today." John was the surgeon who performed the operations on both Dave and I a few years back.

"Have you had that follow up MRI you are supposed to get every two years?" Dave asked in a tone that suggested it wasn't really a question but a statement that he knew I hadn't.

"Not as yet Davey but I will get to it," I replied quietly.

"You ok mate?" He said rather seriously.

"Yes, all good see you on the tee in the morning.' I said not wanting to go into why I sounded the way I did.

As always he was the caddy looking out for me, despite his incredibly busy schedule he made everyone feel as if they were at the front of his mind. So much like a protective big brother, or was it a great uncle I let myself contemplate as I hung up the phone.

17ᵀᴴ HOLE

There are moments that define us. In each round of golf no matter how we have played overall, we can distinguish ourselves with a particular shot or perhaps even more importantly, we project our character in the way we deal with a challenging situation. These instants are fleeting, and though they will always present themselves to you, there are only so many opportunities, so learn and grow from each one. Don't wait until the end to review yourself, do it as you go because the end may not be when or where you expect it to be.

B obby Jones, acclaimed as one of the most cerebral golfers of all time once said,

"Golf is the closest game to the game we call life. You get bad breaks from the good shots, you

get good breaks from the bad shots – but you still
have to play the ball where it lies."

A simple statement from Robert Tyre Jones but as with most profound utterances, the simplicity cleverly contains multi-layered meanings. In golf, you most certainly get a lot of good, and bad breaks and yet golfers tend to focus more on the bad ones. Those bad bounces or unfair lies are seared into their memories and will be spoken about emotionally throughout the round and sometimes for days and weeks afterward building layer upon layer of mental scar tissue. Dave had observed this early in his golf education, and he worked very hard to get his players and his friends to acknowledge the good breaks they were also gifted from this tantalizing and tormenting game, and then use that awareness productively. The ratio of good and bad breaks tended to even out over time but getting most golfers to see it as a balanced account proved arduous. Most people missed the lesson that dealing with the bad situations in a level-headed manner and accepting and using the good luck you receive is part of the beautiful tuition that this game offers, and is one of the most direct correlations with life in general.

I couldn't decide if the discovery of the verse and the connection between my namesake and my closest friend was a good break or a bad break, but as Mr. Jones said, I now had to deal with that knowledge. It could be a nothing more than coincidence that the verse chosen for Davey was explicitly written for my great uncle all those years ago, but it just seemed so improbable and the odds too fantastic to accept or explain it away as pure happenstance. It was even more difficult for me to seriously consider it as a chance event because I genuinely wanted the link to be meaningful and secretly hoped it was deliberate. Premeditated by who and why though, I had no idea. The void of concrete suppositions in my mind left plenty of room for fanciful indulgence.

Private Doug Nanfield had already faced a few dicey moments in combat since arriving in Malaysia seven months earlier. This, however, was a hell storm. The confrontation was unexpected, and his unit was totally unprepared for the intensity of the attack, and despite bravely engaging the enemy and holding them back for a short while, they had no chance. They were outnumbered and outgunned. The loss of so many good men around him, falling again and again in his peripheral vision, made his heart break but at the same time, a raging anger flooded through his entire body and his mind. He felt like he had superhuman power, remarkable considering that exhaustion had been overwhelming him only minutes before. He tore into the opposing line taking out at least a dozen enemy soldiers. It was only when he stopped briefly to help one of his fallen buddies that he provided a few seconds of opportunity to the other side. He felt the hit on his left side, strangely there wasn't any pain, and his first thought was that someone or something heavy had fallen against his left upper leg. It knocked him off his feet. Though when he looked down and saw the blood and mangled flesh of his thigh, he realised what had happened. The noise that had been so loud it had made the ground shudder seemed to drift away into the background, and as the blackness closed in on him, Doug said to himself,

"I thought being shot was going to feel different than that." He heard a voice behind him to the right,

"What are you leaving behind?" his last conscious thought was,

"What a stupid bloody question!!"

He woke up in a dark, moist hut. His head was throbbing, and there was a pulsating pain in his left leg that took his breath away. His mouth and throat were so dry that swallowing and forming words were difficult. His thirst was immense. As he struggled to full consciousness, the stupefying awareness that he was still alive prompted multiple questions in his mind that screamed for believable answers. Sluggishly the comprehension of what must have happened coalesced in his weary mind, and it was confirmed when he heard the sharp staccato of Japanese voices issuing orders outside in single syllables of limited English. He dragged himself painfully over to a wall and through a crack he witnessed the horror of what was actually going on. A small line of Australian soldiers stood blindfolded and one after the other they were ordered to kneel, and they were executed via one blow from a sword expertly wielded by one of the Japanese soldiers who appeared unmoved by his grisly duty. These evil theatrics were performed in front of a couple of hundred prisoners. If one of the condemned men in the line put up any resistance, then the man shouting the orders would fire his pistol indiscriminately into the audience of men being forced to watch this scene. So to protect the rest of their compatriots and allies each man had to accept his fate stoically.

"Why would they bother to capture and bring these men to this camp only to execute them?" Doug thought to himself, "why not kill them on the battlefield?" After watching for a few minutes, he decided it must be to make an example to the rest of the prisoners to deter any resistance and to demonstrate who was in power. He also realised that he would soon be part of the show.

"What will you leave behind to help them?" The soft voice coming from the darkness of the hut startled him.

"I can't help them, and besides I have nothing to leave anyway!" he shouted at the invisible voice, his pain and his fear causing him to cry out louder than he had intended.

"I don't mean these men here; the ones you left behind will need guidance." Doug was confused; did he mean the men in his unit who had been left at the site of the ambush?

Despite not having spoken this question out loud he received a one-word answer.

"Home." It was said calmly but with surety and firmness and Doug knew by the tone that there would be no more conversation. There wasn't any time for further discussion anyway because the door to the hut was rudely thrown open and two armed Japanese soldiers were motioning to him impatiently to move outside.

"It's one of those moments Rod. You can take control of the tournament with one good shot here."

Davey stood in the middle of the fairway on the par 5 17th hole at Royal Melbourne, talking through the upcoming shot with Rod Hazelbrook. They were in the final round of the Australian Open and Rod had a one-shot lead, and his nearest challenger had already finished for the day. If Rod birdied the hole, he would have a two-shot lead, and with the relatively straightforward 18th to finish, the open should be his. Rod's father had recovered well from surgery, and with the chemotherapy now underway he had insisted that his son play the main events on the local tour. At first, his form was inconsistent after the layoff, but this week he was back to his best. Dave knew it was because he was relieved about the improvement in his Dad's health, so he shrewdly decided to 'disengage the stress.'

"The old man looks great doesn't he Rod. Do you reckon they will let us take the trophy into the hospital tonight even though it will be outside visiting hours?" Rod smiled warmly at Dave and then confidently hit his 2 iron into the heart of the green.

"Game over. Now let's hole the eagle putt and leave something behind for these people to remember from today. You go ahead mate take the applause you've earned it, but think about your dad on the walk in, I know he's watching on TV, but he's been here with you every step today."

After sitting in the gloomy hut, the sunlight temporarily obscured his vision. As he refocused, the first thing he saw clearly was the guard motioning to him to put on the blindfold. Doug Nanfield refused the offer; he didn't want the last image he saw in this life to be the back of a dirty rag. Plus he wanted to look these bastards in the eye. He remembered the voice, and he thought about home. He pictured his parents and his sister Joan and his nephews, George and John. He suddenly felt an aching sadness; there was so much he had planned to share with them all, now he was being robbed of that chance, the guilt and sorrow started to well up inside of him. Then he felt the anger rise once more. He wasn't going to die feeling fearful and lost. He summoned all his remaining strength and filled his mind and heart with love for his family, especially the boys. They would need direction given they had already lost their father as a consequence of this devastating war. As he was shoved to his knees he focused even more resolutely; he saw the faces of his nephews,

"I'm here fellas I'll always be close by," Doug said tenderly. He saw young George lift his head and look directly at him. He heard a sound like the flapping of a bird's wing behind him. White Light...

18TH HOLE

Is the end really the end? Or is it merely a pause before a new beginning? As you walk off the 18th green, it's common to tell yourself that this game beats me up too often and maybe I won't play anymore or at least I'll have a break from it. However, the hold this incredible obsession has on us usually wins out, and by the time you've had a post-round drink or driven home, you have begun to plan your improvement strategy for the next round, and the anticipation and excitement starts it's inexorable build up once more. As we approach our twilight years and play the last hole of life, will we stop to think, if I was granted a second chance and could head back to the first tee again, would I play it any differently?

How you feel after the completion of a round of golf or at the end of your life is a culmination of what has happened throughout that time and is influenced by the decisions you made and the actions you've taken. The distinct difference though is that in golf you always have the chance to do it over the next time you play and hopefully apply some of the learnings and perform better and enjoy it more. The one change we should all make is to focus less on the regrets. The golfers' habit is almost always a post-round lament about the mistakes and missed opportunities. It is rare to hear a rapturous tale of the successes and inspiring events from the day, and so many important observations and shared experiences, no matter how minor, are lost forever never to be celebrated. Often the instances that seem insignificant at the time could be the most powerful and lasting. Seeing kangaroos bounding through a bunker as the sun rises and the morning mist floats across the course, being transfixed by an eagle soaring over the 17th tee, witnessing the satisfaction on the face of your mate when he finally executes a textbook bunker shot after years of mental torture in the sand. These are the special moments. Still, we obsess about that three-putt or the hook into the lake. We walk right past the beauty to do battle with the beast.

We only have the one life to get as many things right as we can and make an impact on the world around us and the people we interact with, one chance to leave a legacy behind. Golf thankfully gives us multiple mulligans on the course, but at the same time, it provides by example a broader curriculum for our lives. Of course, we should enjoy the activity, but as we drive down the road, it's important to lift your gaze from the white line once in a while and look out the window.

As the link between my great uncle and Davey became more and more real to me, I frequently wondered why the connection to me came through Dave. Why not my father George? Doug Nanfield was his uncle. I can only assume that the painful, fatherless upbringing in the difficult post-war years affected my Dad tremendously and he found it hard to reveal the side of him that I would have loved to know. We didn't really communicate openly, we both tended to cover up our feelings with superficial humour. His career as a policeman would have been extremely stressful, and he dealt with terrible things that can scar the soul deep down. It is poignant that he took on a career that was all about protecting and helping people in an environment of violence and conflict. The loss and struggle of his early life must have equally caused him to build up emotional barriers as protection. He also bore the brunt of his mother's pain who had lost not only her husband who couldn't face domestic life after returning from Africa and deserted the family, but she would have been tormented by the image she was forced to permanently review in her mind of how her cherished brother was killed. Sadly she took it out on Dad far more than his younger brother John. I've never understood why, but being the oldest and having to take on the role of man of the house and his strong resemblance to his father may have contributed to her resentment. The destructive vestiges of the horror of war span generations. Much as I genuinely respected my father, we never had as close a relationship as I believe both of us needed, and I know that the fault was also partly mine. As I have explored and documented the importance and benefit of having a caddy in golf and life, the realisation that my father and my Nan both needed the soothing steady support of a caddy figure in their lives, weighs heavily on me. I should have known, and I could have taken on that role. But I didn't.

Is it possible that I was closed off to any connection until the appearance of Davey and his help and guidance filled a void in my own life? The portal may have opened up through the acceptance of a close male bond. I am sure the friendship and the mutual love of golf were catalysts, as were the similarities between us. Neither of us had a brother, and we were both the eldest child with younger sisters. Intriguingly my Dad always got on extremely well with Dave, from the very first meeting they clicked and Dad thought a lot of him. Dave had a knack for making my father comfortable, and he would ask him a lot of questions about his past and his career. At parties and family gatherings I would often see them together in a corner; Dad would be in full flow telling stories to Davey who appeared to be enjoying every word, just like old friends catching up.

It is easy enough to pretend that I didn't get any messages or intuition myself, but the truth is I had received some strange communications once or twice, and yet I deliberately dismissed them and cravenly refused to tell anybody. Once when I was cleaning the pool at dusk admiring the pink sunset, I distinctly heard a voice behind me.

"Where's Rose Doug?" I was asked. I turned around, but I was all alone. Rose was the name of my maternal grandmother and the only person I had ever heard call her that was my grandfather who had died 25 years earlier. My grandmother was approaching 100 and had been in a nursing home for many years. I learned later that week that my mother and her sisters had moved Gran to another home a few days before my strange encounter.

On the wall of my study, there is a photograph from our wedding. I adore this picture. It captures the moment perfectly. Olivia and I are radiantly happy, and the natural joy on our faces is apparent to everyone. Davey is also standing there, just the three of us and the photographer. At the last minute after all the official photographs had been taken, we decided to go down the hill and get one last shot as the sun was setting, and it seemed appropriate that it was only us. We had all been through so much, and Davey was the one who had brought the two of us together. I love the look on Davey's face in the shot. He is looking to the side with a happy, satisfied and relaxed expression, almost as if he is acknowledging someone nearby. I had always assumed it was a guest from the wedding party, but for the first time recently a thought occurred to me, I recalled that there wasn't anyone else there at that moment; we were at least a hundred metres away from everyone. Who was he looking at? It wasn't the photographer as he was on the other side. If you focus on Dave on his own in the picture and interpret his body language, it is easy to entertain the idea that he is in an exchange with somebody. It's most likely just me indulging my imagination once more.

How Davey came into my life doesn't matter nearly as much as the impact he has had since arriving. I am grateful and consider myself blessed to have had his counsel and guidance but most of all his friendship. So many times I have been amazed at what he has been able to do for other people, and I have been the fortunate recipient more than most. It is my nature to attempt to analyse why everything happens, to seek the reasons and explanations, but I am beginning to understand that we should just try and enjoy the wonder of what is around us, trusting it without the compulsion to understand the aetiology. Not many of us have advanced knowledge of the technology and natural science around us, other than the rudimentary lessons from school, but we utilise, admire and enjoy the positive elements and tools of our environment every day without question or demands for the blueprints.

There have no doubt been caddy figures in your own lives at different times, maybe you didn't notice, and I am sure like me you haven't fully appreciated them. If you have one cherish them, if you haven't and need one, look around you they're nearby. Most importantly though, try to be one yourself for someone else, that I believe has been my most significant realisation. It's not about who is carrying your bag, but rather whose bag you are willing to sling over your own shoulder!

Dragging my mind back to the logical side, I try to dismiss the idea of people being able to influence events from another realm. But I can't help but think of all the incredible connections and unexplainable coincidences that made me begin to believe that my great uncle Doug Nanfield was reincarnated in Davey or somehow working through him to guide me. And I have to try hard again to quell my emotional leaps of faith with sensible pragmatism. We do only have one life within which we can make our mark and leave something behind,

"Or do we?"

Printed in the United States
By Bookmasters